"Here's To What

His words settled over her like a soft caress. He wrapped her in his embrace and snuggled back into the corner of the couch, pulling her with him.

"It's been a long time, Vicki. I've often wondered what happened to you, what you were doing... whether or not you were happy."

It was not what she had been expecting and she was not sure how to respond. "I was wondering the same thing about you."

Any further thoughts were put on hold when he claimed her mouth with all the passion he had been carrying inside him for the past fifteen years.

A soft moan escaped her lips. Things had gone too far. She could not stop what was happening even if she wanted to. If it was to be that they had only this one night together, then she wanted it to be enough to last her a lifetime.

Dear Reader,

Silhouette Desire is proud to launch three brand-new, emotional and romantic miniseries this month! We've got twin sisters switching places, sexy men who rise above their pasts and a ranching family marrying off their Texas daughters.

Along with our spectacular new miniseries, we're bringing you Anne McAllister's latest novel in her bestselling CODE OF THE WEST series, July's MAN OF THE MONTH selection, *The Cowboy Crashes a Wedding*. Next, a shy, no-frills librarian leads a fairy-tale life when she masquerades as her twin sister in Barbara McMahon's *Cinderella Twin*, book one of her IDENTICAL TWINS! duet. In *Seducing the Proper Miss Miller* by Anne Marie Winston, the town's black sheep and the minister's daughter cause a scandal with their sudden wedding.

Sexy Western author Peggy Moreland invites readers to get to know the McCloud sisters and the irresistible men who court them—don't miss the first TEXAS BRIDES book, *The Rancher's Spittin' Image*. And a millionaire bachelor discovers his secret heir in *The Tycoon's Son* by talented author Shawna Delacorte. A gorgeous loner is keeping quiet about *His Most Scandalous Secret* in the first book in Susan Crosby's THE LONE WOLVES miniseries.

So get to know the friends and families in Silhouette Desire's hottest new miniseries—and watch for more of their love stories in months to come!

Regards,

Melissa Senate

Melissa Senate
Senior Editor
Silhouette Books

Please address questions and book requests to:
Silhouette Reader Service
U.S.: 3010 Walden Ave., P.O. Box 1325, Buffalo, NY 14269
Canadian: P.O. Box 609, Fort Erie, Ont. L2A 5X3

SHAWNA DELACORTE
THE TYCOON'S SON

SILHOUETTE *Desire*®
Published by Silhouette Books
America's Publisher of Contemporary Romance

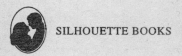

SILHOUETTE BOOKS

ISBN 0-373-76157-0

THE TYCOON'S SON

This edition published by arrangement with Harlequin Books S.A.

® and TM are trademarks of Harlequin Books S.A., used under license. Trademarks indicated with ® are registered in the United States Patent and Trademark Office, the Canadian Trade Marks Office and in other countries.

Printed in U.S.A.

Books by Shawna Delacorte

Silhouette Desire

Sarah and the Stranger #730
The Bargain Bachelor #759
Cassie's Last Goodbye #814
Miracle Baby #905
Cowboy Dreaming #1020
Wyoming Wife? #1110
The Tycoon's Son #1157

Yours Truly

Much Ado About Marriage

SHAWNA DELACORTE

has delayed her move to Washington State, staying in the
Midwest in order to spend some additional time with
family. She still travels as often as time permits and is
looking forward to visiting several new places during the
upcoming year while continuing to devote herself to
writing full-time.

One

Vicki Bingham stood on the porch of the country store. The shiver of trepidation started as a little twinge, then spread throughout her body. After fifteen years, Wyatt Edwards was about to step back into her life.

Hunching her shoulders against the cold tremor that engulfed her, she stared up at the empty house standing in stately grandeur on top of the hill. It seemed to look across the valley and out to the ocean like a dark, brooding monarch surveying his kingdom. No one from the Edwards family had lived in the house since the death of Henry Edwards ten years ago. And now it was about to be occupied again by Wyatt, Henry's only child.

Her ever increasing anxiety forced her to look away. Nothing good could come from this, but she did not know what to do about it.

"Victoria Dalton Bingham!"

Vicki stiffened at the sound of her name. She recognized the voice immediately. It had the same quality as chalk squeaking on a blackboard and affected her the same way. Alice Thackery, a prim woman in her early sixties, was the town busybody and self-appointed guardian of everyone's morals. Vicki forced a smile and turned around to face the unavoidable.

"Yes, Mrs. Thackery, what can I do for you?" She could tell by the woman's pinched expression and tightly pursed lips that she was about to be involved in yet another unpleasant confrontation.

"I realize, Victoria, that you had to make certain adjustments when you returned to Sea Cliff to run the store after your father died, but you've been here for two months now and I feel that's long enough. I've mentioned this to you on numerous occasions in an attempt to be a good neighbor, but you seem determined to ignore all my attempts to be gracious in this matter." Mrs. Thackery shifted her shopping basket from one arm to the other as she waited for a response.

Vicki allowed a sigh of resignation. "What seems to be the problem this time, Mrs. Thackery?"

"It's that boy of yours. You're allowing that teenage hooligan to run wild around the streets and I won't have it!"

Vicki stretched herself to her full five-foot-seven-inch height and glared down at the shorter woman. She took a calming breath, determined to control her temper. "I will thank you to stop referring to my son as a 'teenage hooligan.' Richie is no such thing. He's a healthy, normal boy who needs his exercise. He's not a troublemaker and does not run wild around the streets."

"Not an hour ago, Victoria, he came speeding around the corner on that two-wheeled contraption of his and nearly ran into me. He was with that Forsythe boy and everyone in town knows that little hooligan is just a breath away from reform school."

"That 'two-wheeled contraption' is a bicycle—a dirt bike—not some high-powered motorcycle."

Mrs. Thackery turned to leave, but not before delivering a parting shot. "Nonetheless, I expect him to control the way he charges around the streets. Humph! It's getting so a decent person isn't safe walking along the sidewalk."

Vicki went inside the store, a combination market and post office. She slammed the screen door harder than she intended.

"What's the matter, Mom?"

Her son's voice caught her by surprise. She whirled around and spotted him coming out of the back office with a handful of cookies. "Richie...how long have you been here?" She knew the upheaval in his life had been very difficult for her son. When her husband, Robert Bingham, had died five years ago it had been devastating for Richie. Then, two months ago, he had been uprooted once again when they moved from Dallas, Texas, to the small rural community of Sea Cliff on the northern California coast. She was thankful school had started so that at least he could make some new friends.

He popped one of the cookies into his mouth, practically inhaling it rather than eating it. "I don't know...five minutes, I guess." He shoved another cookie into his mouth. "Me and Tim—"

"Tim and I." She brushed the hair back from his forehead.

"Cut it out, Mom." A spark of irritation showed as he backed away from her motherly fussing. "*Tim and I* were riding on this great trail he knows back in the hills." He took a soft drink from the refrigerator.

"You were also zipping around the sidewalks." She started to tell him to put back the soft drink and not eat any more cookies because he would spoil his dinner, but they would have been wasted words. At fourteen-and-a-half, he had the voracious appetite of a garbage-disposal unit. He was growing so fast that he could consume what seemed like huge amounts of food and immediately burn it up. He was already as tall as she was and seemed to be all legs. He would eventually top six feet, easily.

He shot her a look of disgust. "Yeah... I saw old lady Thackery leavin'. It wasn't like she said."

"That's *Mrs.* Thackery. And what she said was that you nearly ran her down with your bike."

"No way! We were riding in the street, not on the sidewalk. She was standing in her yard. We weren't even close to her!" He dropped his voice almost to a whisper and stared at the floor, talking more to himself than to his mother. "That old lady's a menace to society." He looked up and met her gaze. "Did you know her from when you used to live here?"

"Oh, yes." Vicki gazed upward, as if asking for protection against some sort of recurring menace. A hint of weariness crept into her voice. "I think Mrs. Thackery has lived here forever."

She saw the look of defiance on her son's face. It was a look she knew so well from many years ago, a look that used to cross another handsome young man's face...a handsome young man with the same dark hair and intense, sky-blue eyes. She reached out to smooth his hair again, but stopped when she saw the look, the one that said *Don't mess with my hair and stop treating me like a kid.* "Have you done your homework?"

"Yeah, it's done." He popped another cookie into his mouth. "When's dinner?"

Each time a truck passed Vicki's door on the way up the hill it signaled that the moment she dreaded had moved that much closer. The construction phase of the remodeling had been completed a couple of days earlier. The landscapers had finished on schedule. Moving vans had been delivering both new items and things from a storage company for the past two days. There did not seem to be anything left...only the arrival of Wyatt Edwards.

The local gossip mill had pegged his arrival for the next day, which meant that she had less than twenty-four hours to prepare herself. She did not have any idea what she would say to Wyatt Edwards or what to expect from him. He had walked out on her fifteen years ago, left while she was away for the weekend so that he did not have to face her with his decision. She had been devastated. She could still hear Henry Edwards telling her that she had driven his son away with her constant demands for his attention, until he had not been able to take it anymore.

She had not understood what Henry Edwards had meant at the time. In fact, she still did not understand. It was Wyatt who had been the aggressor, who had pursued her in spite of objections from both their families. She shook her head in an attempt to shove away the bad memories. It was ancient history and no longer relevant to her life. She had a son to take care of and he was more important to her than anything else.

Vicki went about her business for the rest of the day, making a valiant attempt to put the imminent arrival of Wyatt Edwards out of her mind. That evening she helped Richie with a school project for his English class.

Unfortunately, all her attempts at keeping busy did not help. Once she had climbed into bed, turned out the light and closed her eyes, her mind immediately filled with thoughts and memories from long ago. She finally drifted into an uneasy sleep, but woke up several times during the night, the last time being only half an hour before her alarm was set to wake her. She stared at the glowing numerals for five minutes, then with a heavy sigh of resignation reluctantly climbed out of bed. It was a day she would rather not have to face, but she knew there was no way of avoiding it.

She fixed breakfast, and sent Richie off to the school bus. Then she sat down and stared at the clock. In thirty minutes the truck would drop off the day's mail to be sorted and placed in the individual post-office boxes. She forced herself into action, knowing that the moment she'd dreaded would soon be at hand.

Wyatt Edwards pulled his car to the side of the road and turned off the engine. Only five more miles to the Sea Cliff turnoff. It was the first time he had been back since his father's death ten years ago when he had inherited controlling interest in his father's worldwide industrial holdings. He still was not sure exactly what had prompted the decision, but it was too late to turn back now. He had already spent a great deal of money on making the old house livable and preparing an office wing. He planned to conduct most of his business from there, venturing into San Francisco to the corporate headquarters only a few days a month.

He looked out over the ocean, watching as the waves crashed against the rocks just offshore, then climbed out of his car and walked to the edge of the cliff. The small sandy cove below was the place where he and Vicki Dalton had made love for the first and only time. It had been an impetuous action following a beach party. The next day they both agreed that they had acted foolishly. It had been a very profound experience for him and had solidified in his mind just how much he loved her, even though he had never told her so.

Every minute of that night remained etched in his memory and the emotions associated with it had not diminished over the ensuing years. Even though it had been fifteen years since he had seen or talked to her, he had never been able to shake Vicki from his mind...or from his heart.

He clenched his jaw. Neither could he shake the pain of returning home from a last-minute emergency business trip to South America to find she had moved away without leaving him so much as a note. Then, a month later, he had heard that she was married. It was a memory that still angered him as much as it had when he first heard about it—and also filled him with sorrow for what might have been.

He picked up a rock and threw it as far out as he could, watching as it fell to the ocean below. He picked up another rock and repeated the exercise. He kicked at a third rock, sending it over the edge of the bluff, followed by a cloud of dust. He turned his back on the ocean view, but he could not turn his back on his memories. Finally he climbed into his car and continued down the highway.

He turned onto Sea Cliff Road and was immediately struck that everything looked exactly as it had the last time he was there. Forsythe's gas station still had the Full Service sign next to the pump, even though they had stopped giving full service almost twenty years ago. It appeared that nothing in Sea Cliff had changed. Then his gaze settled on the general store.

That store, a house a block away, and a couple of acres of land were all that Willis Dalton had left. Vicki's father and his own father, Henry Edwards, had been bitter enemies. Their feud had started when Willis's and Henry's respective fathers had had a falling out over a business deal gone bad. Wyatt's grandfather had ended up the winner and Vicki's grandfather had lost almost everything.

Wyatt and Vicki had defied both sets of parents by dating and falling in love—at least Wyatt had thought they were in love. But obviously he had been wrong about Vicki Dalton's feelings for him. He wrinkled his brow in irritation at the fact that it still bothered him. After all these years it was still a thorn in his side.

He pulled his car into a parking space next to the post-office entrance at the back of the general store. He needed to make arrangements for a post-office box. He entered the building and looked around. No one was there. He walked through the connecting door to the market that occupied the front of the building.

Shock hit him smack in the face. He stopped dead in his tracks. It could not be.

Vicki Dalton was standing behind the counter by the front door. It took him a few seconds to collect his wits and recover his composure. He stared at her, noting the way she bit at her lower lip. It was a nervous little habit that had always manifested itself whenever she was upset or worried about something. As he watched her, he felt a soft warmth flicker to life. She looked every bit as beautiful as the image he had carried in his mind all these years.

He quickly ducked out of sight. He certainly had not planned on this. He had been prepared for the unpleasant and awkward necessity of dealing with Willis Dalton, but not for the reality of seeing Vicki again. It was not too late; there was still time. She had not seen him yet. He could turn around and drive back to San Francisco. He drew a steadying breath. He needed to gather his wits about him. Then a surge of anger brought him back to reality.

No, he would not turn and run. She had disappeared from his life fifteen years ago and he had never known why. He clenched his jaw in renewed determination. He could not leave until he had confronted her and demanded an explanation. He wanted her to know exactly how much pain she had caused him—how much pain he had been carrying all these years. He stepped back through the door into the market.

"Well, well, well..." He took a couple of steps toward the counter, trying to keep his voice and manner as casual as possible. "If it isn't Vicki Dalton. Only I guess it's not Dalton anymore, is it? It's been a long time, Vicki."

The smooth, masculine voice resonated across the room. She did not need to look up to know its owner's identity. The moment she dreaded had finally arrived. She bit at her lower lip as she continued to stare at the order form she had been filling out. His footsteps pounded in her ears as he drew closer and closer until finally he stood directly in front of her.

"Just how long has it been? Ten years...fifteen?" There was no mistaking the edge to his voice and the antagonism just beneath the surface. "I'm surprised to find you here. Are you just visiting your father or did you decide to move back to Sea Cliff?"

She put down her pen and finally lifted her gaze, smothering the gasp just before it escaped her mouth. His commanding presence overwhelmed her. He seemed to have grown even taller than the six-foot-one height she remembered, and his blue eyes immediately captured her very soul. The bright colors of his sweater enhanced his golden tan. His dark hair was tousled, probably windblown, giving him a very sexy appearance. His features had matured from the boyish good looks she had known. With the passage of time he had become even more handsome...if that was possible.

When she was an inexperienced eighteen, Wyatt Edwards had been an older man of twenty-two. But now she was thirty-three years old, a widow with the responsibility of raising her son by herself, and the proprietor of a business vital to the small community. There were days when she felt a great deal older.

She managed to find her voice, but could not find any of the words she had been rehearsing for two days. Instead, she stammered, more like an impressionable teenager than a mature woman, "Uh...my father... died two months ago. I came back here to run the store. And it's Bingham...Vicki Bingham."

She saw the surprise dart through his eyes, then quickly disappear. His voice softened a little, dropping a bit of its hard edge. "I'm sorry, I didn't know about your father."

"Well…it was sudden. A heart attack." Nervousness churned in the pit of her stomach. She wished a customer would come in or that Noreen Dillon, her full-time employee, would show up for work early— anything to break up the awkwardness that filled the air. She went to the magazine rack and began straightening the periodicals. She felt his stare follow her every movement, but refused to turn and look at him while she spoke. "My…uh…father had mentioned something several years ago about your father passing away. It seems to me that he said your mother had moved back East somewhere."

"Yes, Mother returned to her hometown of Boston. She still lives there."

"What brings you to Sea Cliff?" She was not sure why she had asked such an inane question. He had to know that everyone in the small town would be talking about the renovations to the family house and would have seen the moving vans.

"I'm moving back into the house."

"I see." She still refused to look at him. She straightened the last magazine in the rack and returned to the counter.

"Vicki…" The edge returned to his voice, now impatient. "I'm trying to conduct some business here and I'd appreciate it if I could have your attention for a few minutes."

She was not sure what he was talking about, but she did not like the sound of it. Her defenses went on full alert. "All you need to do is pick out your purchases and bring them here to the counter and I'll be glad to ring them up for you." She bit at her lower lip and twirled a strand of hair around her finger as she glanced around the market.

Wyatt did not understand her blatantly obvious nervousness. He could have understood a show of guilt on her part—she certainly had lots to feel guilty about—but this was different. She appeared almost obsessed with finding mindless little things to do and went out of her way to avoid any eye contact with him.

He took a deep breath and held it for a moment. He would have to save the speculation for some other time, after he had an opportunity to digest all the unexpected happenings of the morning. He adopted a businesslike manner and tried to project an authoritative tone of voice. "I want to make arrangements for a post-office box."

Her gaze flew to meet his. He noted a strange combination of surprise and…well, *relief* was the only word he could find that seemed to fit. It was a very odd reaction on her part, one he found strangely out of place.

"A post-office box? That's why you're here?"

"This," he gestured toward the back of the building, "is the post office, isn't it? And I assume you are the official agent for the United States Postal Service." He fixed her with a hard stare.

Antagonistic…that was the word that immediately leapt to Vicki's mind. Why was he being so antagonistic? If anyone had a right to exhibit hostility and anger, it certainly was not Wyatt Edwards. She drew in a calming breath, then slowly let it out. "Yes, of course."

She led the way to the post office at the back of the building. Wyatt stepped through the customer entrance while Vicki went through the employee door. She reached below the counter and withdrew a form. "Here," she said, shoving it through the customer window toward Wyatt. "Fill this out and sign it."

"I'll require one medium-size box for my personal mail and a large-size box in the corporation's name."

She checked the list of available boxes while he filled out the form. "Here are the two keys. Please try them before you leave to make sure they work." She slid the keys through the window, and allowed her hand to linger on them while she looked over the form he had completed.

Wyatt reached for the keys, but halted as soon as he focused on her left hand. She wore no ring, nor was there any indication that she had recently worn one. His brow was furrowed as he slid the keys out from under her fingers.

He located the two boxes and tried both keys. "Everything seems to be okay." He returned to the customer window where Vicki waited. "What time of day is the mail available for pickup?"

The conversation continued for a few minutes—innocuous questions about the daily mail, the hours of operation for the market, and about placing orders for specialty items from time to time. The sound of a buzzer interrupted them, indicating that someone had entered the market.

"I'll be right there," Vicki called out to the unknown person, then turned her attention back to Wyatt. "Is there anything else you want before I go?"

"Yes, there is." He leveled a soul-searching gaze at her. "I want to know what happened to your wedding ring."

"My...my wedding ring?" A hard lump formed in

her throat and the nervousness churned in her stomach again. Why would he ask such a question?

"Yes. I couldn't help but notice you're not wearing one."

She heard it in his voice again. Antagonism... accusation...the hint of some hidden knowledge. Did he know she had a son? Did he know about Richie? She looked down at her hand, stared at the finger where she had worn the simple gold band Robert Bingham had placed there on their wedding day. She felt the anxious tremor and swallowed hard in an attempt to bring her feelings under control. She knew she had to be very careful how she responded to his question.

"My ring..." She again stared at her hand. "I lost my husband in a plane crash. I'm a widow."

She saw the shock cover his face. She saw something else, too—something in his eyes that she could not identify. Resentment? Smug satisfaction? She did not know.

"A widow?" Wyatt could not hide his reaction to this latest revelation. He had come back to a quiet little town where nothing ever happened and in fifteen minutes had been hit with one shock after another. He had not anticipated seeing Vicki at all, but she was there. Then he had learned about her father's recent death, and now this—what else could there possibly be? How many more surprises were just waiting to jump out at him?

"You'll have to excuse me, I have a customer to tend to." Vicki quickly left the post office and hurried toward the front of the market. "Yes, may I help you with something?"

Wyatt tuned out the voices coming from the market.

Her sudden and extreme nervousness had immediately grabbed his attention—the way she bit at her lower lip, how her face had seemed to pale and her hand tremble at the mention of her wedding ring. He suspected she was hiding something and he was determined to find out what it was.

His assumption had been that she was divorced, and he had intended to make some type of caustic remark to the effect that her decision to run off and get married hadn't been a good one. But this was different. She was a widow. He did not want to delve into her personal life under these circumstances—at least not at that moment. He had started to extend the obligatory condolences, but the words caught in his throat.

He moved to the connecting door and watched as Vicki's customer left the market. He stuck his post-office-box keys in his pocket, stepped through the door and took a steadying breath in the hopes of concealing his reaction. "I guess I'm pretty much out of touch with things around here. You said a plane crash?"

She averted her gaze, once again unable to maintain eye contact with him. "Yes. It...uh...was five years ago." She felt very uncomfortable with the task of explaining her husband's death to Wyatt Edwards. If Wyatt had not walked out on her, none of this ever would have happened. *What if...* She had played that game too many times. "It was a small private plane. Robert was the passenger. It went down in a field about ten miles from our home in Dallas."

"Oh." *Oh...* It was a dumb thing for him to say, but he did not seem to be able to come up with the right words. As much as he had hoped that she had been every bit as miserable as he had been for the past fifteen years, he had not anticipated this. He wanted to know so much, he wanted to know everything, but he could not bring himself to ask. "Well...I guess I'd better be going. I have several things to do. I need to unpack..." His voice trailed off and he finally turned and left without saying anything else.

Vicki closed her eyes and sank back against the wall in an effort to compose herself. Her meeting with Wyatt had been a thousand times worse than she thought it would be. It almost seemed as if he had gone out of his way to be contrary and she did not understand why. *He* had walked out on her, not the other way around. *She* had been the injured party, the one with every right to be angry.

She knew there was no way they could avoid each other in the normal course of day-to-day activities in the small community, but she vowed to make sure everything stayed on an impersonal level. For the sake of her son, Wyatt Edwards could not be allowed back into her life.

The sound of the door shook her from her disturbing thoughts.

"Good morning, Vicki." Noreen's cheerful personality filled the store. "Looks like it's going to be another beautiful day. I love this time of year—the last warmth of summer changing over to the crispness of autumn."

"Good morning." Vicki marveled at the way Noreen always managed to be in such a good mood. A woman in her early forties who had never been married, she always bubbled with good cheer. It seemed that nothing ever upset her.

As he drove up the hill to his house, Wyatt furrowed his brow in concentration. Something strange was going on. Vicki appeared far too nervous. She was hiding something. Did it have to do with him? Was the story about her husband dying in a place crash something she had made up in order to hide the truth?

Get a grip. You're beginning to sound paranoid. This isn't some sort of mystery novel. It's just one of those weird little quirks of life—nothing more.

He did his best to rationalize what had happened. Things were bound to be awkward between them, considering their past history and what she had done to him. He considered himself a mature adult who certainly knew how to handle an uncomfortable situation. He had brought those skills into play often enough in his business dealings. And this was no different. At least that was what he tried to tell himself, even though he knew it wasn't true. This was not business. It was personal—very personal.

Two

Wyatt drove through the large gated entrance and parked in the circular drive in front of the house. He looked up at the imposing two-story structure with its gleaming white paint, dark green shutters and roof, and the large verandah that spanned the front and sides of the house. A little tremor of anxiety jittered inside him. It had been ten years since he had set foot in the house. Now, more than ever, he wondered if he had made a colossal error in deciding to return.

"Wasn't it Thomas Wolfe who said, 'You can't go home again'?" He said the words aloud to no one in particular. Perhaps Thomas Wolfe had been correct. He climbed out of the car, grabbed his suitcase, and walked up the front steps to the large oak double doors.

Just inside the front door he stopped and looked around. The house was elegant to the point of almost being out of place in such a rural setting. The foyer was two stories high, with a large crystal chandelier that hung from the cathedral ceiling. A curved oak staircase traveled up each side to a second-floor landing that looked down on the entrance. He had designated the ground-floor east wing as his office area. The west wing included the den, the billiards room and a small study that had been his father's personal domain.

The formal living room, dining room and kitchen facilities were located straight back through the foyer, with servants' quarters beyond the kitchen. The second floor consisted of a large master bedroom suite and a library on one side of the landing and guest rooms on the other side.

Fred Olson, the caretaker who had stayed on all the years that the property had remained vacant, lived in a small apartment above the three-car garage.

It was far too big a house just for Wyatt, but it had been in the family from his great-grandfather's time. He had been approached on several occasions over the last few years by real-estate developers. They had offered him a lot of money for the land, but he had turned down all offers. He was not even sure why. Perhaps it had to do with family honor and tradition. More likely the house represented a time in his past that he did not want to lose—a time when Vicki was part of his life and he had assumed also a part of his future.

So, the large house on the hill had remained empty, silently standing watch over the valley below and the ocean beyond.

Wyatt ascended the staircase to the second floor. He had lots to do and the clock was ticking. He devoted the rest of his day to unpacking and organizing, with the hope that keeping busy would occupy his mind so that his thoughts would not turn toward Vicki. So far the plan had been a dismal failure.

In her store at the base of the hill, Vicki, too, tried to keep active. But her attention shifted to the window every time she heard a car door slam, the accompanying adrenaline surge telling her how frightened she was about the prospect of having Wyatt around all the time. Sometimes Noreen's overabundance of good cheer got on her nerves, but not today. She encouraged her employee's ongoing chatter, welcoming anything that kept her from thinking about Wyatt Edwards.

The day passed far too slowly. Each minute seemed like an hour. Richie visited the store after school, but she immediately sent him home to do his schoolwork. She did not want to risk Wyatt returning and running into her son...*their* son.

She had been almost four months pregnant with Wyatt's child when she had married another man. Robert Bingham knew she needed a stable home for her baby. He also knew she was not in love with him, but he said it did not matter. He had stood by her through a very difficult pregnancy. He had treated her with respect and unconditional love, and he could not have loved her son more if the boy had been his own, never once asking her about Richie's biological father.

Vicki had an overwhelming respect for Robert and with time had grown to love him, too. But it was not the type of passionate, all-consuming love she had felt for Wyatt Edwards—a love that had never vanished from her consciousness. She had never been able to give Robert the kind of love that he had deserved, and it had hurt her each time she saw in his eyes that he knew there would always be someone else. He had never confronted her about it, but she had carried the self-inflicted guilt and the sorrow for the duration of their marriage.

And now her son's real father had unexpectedly reappeared in her life. That posed a tremendous threat to her emotional security and that of her son. She needed to make sure nothing upset Richie's memories of the loving and kind man he knew as his father.

That night as she lay in bed, Vicki was very restless, tossing and turning without getting much sleep. Morning finally came and she forced herself out of bed, leaving a tangled mess of sheets and blankets. Was this how it would be from now on? Would each day begin with an overwhelming fear that her most closely guarded secret would become public knowledge? That Wyatt would discover he had a son? That Richie's world would crash around him even further than it already had? And all the while she would be looking at Wyatt and thinking *what if?*

"Come on, Richie." She knocked on his bedroom door for the second time. "Get out of bed. You're going to miss the school bus if you don't hurry." She heard the irritation in her voice and immediately admonished herself for letting it show.

A moment later the door opened and Richie appeared, dressed and ready for breakfast. He gave her a curious look. She impulsively pulled him into a hug and kissed his forehead.

He quickly squirmed from her arms and stepped back, making no effort to hide his exasperation. "Cut it out! What's the matter with you today?"

She saw the embarrassment that covered his features, the same features that adorned Wyatt's face. She smiled and started to reach for his hair, but stopped when he shot her *the look*. "Nothing's wrong. I'm just glad to see you, that's all."

"Sure, Mom." A withering sigh surrounded his words. "I'm glad to see you, too." His expression said he knew she had totally flipped out and senility had finally set in. He headed for the kitchen, gulped down a glass of orange juice, then reached for the box of cereal.

Vicki hurried to work, arriving early so that she could take care of part of the morning routine in the store before the truck delivered the daily mail. She would be working alone until two o'clock when Noreen came to work. She sorted the mail, finishing just in time to make coffee and unlock the front door to the market.

She heard the bell that signaled that the outside door of the post office had been opened. Most likely someone wanted to check the mail before going to work. She turned to pour herself a cup of coffee. When she turned back, she found Wyatt standing in the connecting door, staring at her. The intense expression on his face sent a shiver of anxiety through her.

"Uh...good morning. I'm surprised to see you again so soon." She took a sip of her coffee to avoid further conversation.

"I just came by to check on my mail," Wyatt said. It was a feeble lie. They both knew there was no way he could have received any mail at his new post-office box yet. He slowly made his way across the store, pausing to look at whatever happened to catch his eye en route, until finally he arrived at the front counter.

He leaned on the countertop and proffered what he hoped was a casual smile. "That coffee smells good."

She indicated the large urn at the end of the counter. "Cups are on the other side, three sizes with the prices marked."

He took a large cup from the dispenser. "I see you have pastries, too. I'll take one of these bear claws to go with my coffee." He placed his money on the counter and she rang up the sale.

The stress level inside Vicki increased dramatically. What did he want from her? Why did he insist on hanging around? She tried to maintain a businesslike manner. "Did you need something else or will that be all?"

He watched as she nervously bit at her lower lip. Her discomfort showed in the way she kept shifting her weight from one foot to the other. Her gaze constantly darted around the market, not staying on any one thing for more than a second or two.

He took a swallow from his coffee cup, deliberately stalling before his response. "Are you expecting someone?"

"Uh...no. No one in particular. Why do you ask?"

"You keep glancing out the window. I just thought maybe you were expecting a delivery or something." Her behavior continued to be what he considered strange, at least for the Vicki Dalton he once knew— back before his whole world turned upside down on him.

He was now more convinced than ever that she was hiding some kind of secret and he was determined to find out what it was. In spite of the fact that she had hurt him and left him empty and angry, she had remained the one and only woman he truly wanted.

Now, for reasons he did not clearly understand, they had been thrown together again. He had a second chance and he was not going to let it go without a fight. He would find out exactly what had happened all those years ago when she walked out on him.

"Vicki..." He saw the way she jumped at the sound of his voice. "Are you all right? I've never seen you so jittery." His words came out as half concern and half irritation.

The buzzer intruded into their conversation once again. Someone had opened the front door of the market. Vicki breathed a sigh of relief as she turned to see who it was. Her relief immediately turned to anxiety when she saw Alice Thackery.

Wyatt eyed the disagreeable woman. He lowered his voice so that only Vicki could hear him. "We'll continue this conversation later. I want to get out of here before she pins me to the wall about something I might have done twenty-five years ago." He nodded curtly to Alice, acknowledging her presence as he left.

Alice watched him until he was out of sight, then turned toward Vicki. Her tightly pursed lips only added to the harshness of her unsmiling features. Her tone was sarcastic and condemning. "Well, I see it didn't take long for Henry's boy to come sniffing around here."

Vicki refused to acknowledge her comment. "Is there something I can help you with, Mrs. Thackery?"

The woman ignored Vicki's question, preferring to continue with her train of thought. "He has *live-in* servants up there, you know." She divulged the information as if she were gossiping about some sort of illicit behavior. "No reason for him to be doing his own marketing." She pointedly stared at Vicki, as if waiting for her to answer some sort of unspoken accusation.

By no stretch of anybody's imagination did Vicki feel she owed Alice Thackery any type of explanation, nor did she have any intention of giving her one. She stood her ground, determined to wait it out.

The awkward silence lasted for several seconds before Alice finally became flustered and grabbed the nearest thing to her without even looking to see what she had picked up. She plopped it on the counter with an exaggerated flair. "I'll take this."

"Are you sure?"

Alice refused to look at the item she had placed on the counter, as if to do so would have cast doubt on her selection. She pursed her lips in a hard line as she stared straight ahead. "I'm sure."

Vicki suppressed a grin as she rang up the sale for a package of bubble gum. She could not stop that same grin from turning up the corners of her mouth as she watched Alice Thackery huff out of the market and down the sidewalk, passing the sheriff's station and volunteer fire department on the way toward her house in the next block. Then the smile slowly faded.

Apprehension shuddered through her. She had the uncomfortable feeling that the disagreeable busybody was going to be responsible for causing her a lot of problems. If anyone would be able to spot the distinct physical resemblance between Wyatt and Richie, it would be Alice Thackery. Vicki could almost feel the dark clouds gathering overhead.

Thankfully, the rest of the morning passed with business as usual, until about eleven o'clock.

"Vicki." Wyatt stepped through the connecting door, his sudden appearance startling her. His voice held an air of absolute authority. "I think we should finish our conversation now."

Her nerves were pulled about as taut as they could be without snapping. Wyatt, Mrs. Thackery and now Wyatt again. Would this day never end? She took a steadying breath before looking in the direction of Wyatt's voice. "What conversation was that?" He was at her side before she was even aware that he had moved.

His manner softened, but there was still an antagonistic edge to his voice. "The one where I was about to ask you to have lunch with me. We could talk over *old times* and catch up on what's been going on without interruptions from your customers."

She closed her eyes for a moment as she tried to collect the panic welling inside her and shove it back into some out-of-the-way corner. Was it her imagination or had he added extra emphasis to the words *old times?* The last thing she wanted to discuss with Wyatt Edwards was *old times.* "I couldn't possibly have lunch with you. I have to be here. Noreen doesn't come to work until two o'clock." She hurried over to the magazine rack and began straightening the periodicals, just as she had done the day before.

He stood behind her, reached over her shoulder, and took the magazine from her hand. He replaced it on the rack, then grabbed her shoulders and turned her around to face him. He leveled a stern look at her. "I don't know what's going on here, Vicki, but we have to talk. We need to clear the air about—" He felt her body stiffen and saw the way her eyes filled with a very real fear that he did not understand—a fear that threatened to turn into all-out panic.

She shook loose from his grasp, determination on

her face as she stepped back from him. "I...I'm very busy here. I don't have time to talk about unimportant things."

"Unimportant things?" He felt a stab of anger that carried over into his voice. She had walked out on him, and he wanted to know why, needed to know why—*had* to know why. "I'm talking about us—about what happened fifteen years ago."

She turned away so that she did not have to look at him. She could not keep the anger out of her voice. "The past is just that, Wyatt. It's the past. It's over and done and can't be changed. Now, if you'll excuse me..." She walked away from him without waiting for a response.

How dare he try to dredge up all the pain and humiliation he put her through fifteen years ago! He had walked out on her without so much as a goodbye note. He hadn't even waited around long enough to discover that she was pregnant with his child. She was afraid to look back, afraid her anger and her newly opened wounds would cause her to blurt out that most closely guarded and important secret of her life.

"It's not over, Vicki. And it won't be over until things are settled between us. I want answers—"

She whirled around and glared at him. Fifteen years of pent-up emotion tried to get out just as desperately as she tried to keep it under control. It was a toss-up as to which would win. She did not want a confrontation with him, she just wanted him to leave her alone. "Drop it, Wyatt. Let it die a quiet and well-deserved death." Her words were strained, and she turned away again before she said something she would regret.

He grabbed her arm and spun her back to him. "I

have no intention of leaving it alone, not until I'm satisfied that things are finally settled.''

"Settled?" She felt her eyes widen in shock. She could not believe what she was hearing. "There's nothing to settle.''

He had tried to forget her, to put what she had done to him out of his mind, but he had never quite been able to accomplish it. She had disappeared out of his life without so much as a word, and had never made any attempt to contact him. He never understood why she had gone away. Then he heard she had married. That news had crushed every hope he had secretly harbored that she would some day return so they could be together again—until now.

Vicki did not even have time to catch her breath before he pulled her into his arms. At first his embrace was somewhat tentative, but he quickly gained confidence. Memories came flooding back, every feeling she ever had for him ignited deep inside her. She immediately shoved away from him, but not in time. His embrace had made a shambles of her self-control. His sky-blue eyes had the smoky blue she remembered so well, conveying the depth of his passion. It was shockingly apparent that the physical pull between them was still as strong as ever, much to her dismay.

"No, it's not settled, Vicki. It's a long way from being settled.'' Then Wyatt turned and walked out the door.

A very shaken Vicki staggered backward a couple more steps, finally bumping into the counter. Her heart pounded so hard that she had trouble catching her breath. Everything she had so desperately tried to erase from her life had resurfaced with astonishing clarity. Wyatt Edwards seemed to have more control over her emotions than she did. His embrace left her with the uncomfortable feeling of being helpless...and extremely vulnerable.

It took a huge effort to pull herself together and continue with her workday, but somehow she managed it.

At two o'clock Noreen arrived promptly for work. "Good afternoon, Vicki."

"Hi, Noreen. Things are pretty quiet around here. I think I'll run home for a little while. I should be back in a couple of hours." Vicki grabbed her purse from beneath the counter and called over her shoulder as she left the market, "If you need me before that, give me a call."

Vicki hurried the one block to her house. She went directly to her bedroom, shut the door, then sat on the edge of her bed. She hugged her shoulders in an attempt to make her body stop trembling. She could still feel his arms around her. It had affected her the same way it had when he held her close fifteen years ago. She needed to pull her emotions together and somehow find a way to deal with this latest emotional upheaval in her life.

If only there had been some sort of warning, she could have done something to prepare herself. But now it was too late. She had once again felt the passion of Wyatt Edwards and knew in an instant how much she had missed his touch.

She went to her closet and stared at the small locked box on the top shelf. After what seemed like an eternity, she took it from the shelf and set it on the bed. She paused a minute, uncertain about whether or not she really wanted to open it, then retrieved the key and unlocked it. She carefully removed a stack of photographs, taking one and putting the others back in the box. She stared at it for a long time. It was a picture of Wyatt and her at a party, the night they had ended up making love on the beach.

It was the night their son had been conceived.

She closed her eyes as she held the photograph to her heart. In a barely audible voice she whispered the feelings that she had tried so desperately to bury. "I've tried to purge you from my existence, erase the memory of what I thought we once meant to each other. But, God help me, I haven't been able to do it."

She forced away the tears that tried to well in her eyes. It had been a little less than a month after the photo was taken that Wyatt had disappeared from her life. His father said Wyatt had felt smothered by her. She tried to think, tried to put herself back in that place again. Was it possible that she had unconsciously made emotional demands on him following their night of lovemaking? She had not meant to. Making love had been as much her responsibility as it had been his.

She shook her head. She did not know what had happened.

She replaced the photograph, locked the box, and put it back on the shelf. Then she did something she had never done before. Rather than going back to work, she poured herself a glass of wine and took it to the glass-walled back porch.

She sat all alone and sipped her wine while she thought about the future. She had handled the shock of losing her mother when she was still in high school, of Wyatt leaving her, of discovering she was pregnant with Wyatt's child, of her husband dying and now her father's death. She did not know if she had enough strength left to endure any more—and that most certainly included Wyatt's sudden reappearance in her life.

Richie had been without a father and role model during his formative adolescent years. He would soon be fifteen. Somehow she had to find a way to make everything work out while seeing to it that her son was protected from any more emotional upheavals. She sat quietly on the porch, vacillating between memories from the past, the problems of the present, and her fears of what the future held.

"Mom! What are you doing home?"

Richie's voice startled her. She had not heard him come in. She glanced at her watch. "Oh...I didn't realize it was so late." She looked over at her son, who was standing in the doorway. "I just needed a little break from work, that's all." She stood up, taking her empty wineglass with her. "I'd better get back to the store. You get busy on your homework and I'll start dinner in a couple of hours."

"I don't have any homework. I did it all at school."

Vicki looked skeptically at him. "How did you manage that?"

"Mrs. Winters had some kind of emergency and had to leave, so my last class was just a study hall. I did everything then." Richie turned toward the door. "So, I'm going to ride on the trail in the hills."

"Okay, but be sure you're back in two hours." She called after him as he ran out the door, "You stay away from Mrs. Thackery's house. I don't want her complaining to me again."

Wyatt had tried to force himself to work all afternoon, but he could not concentrate on anything other than the feel of having Vicki in his arms once again. It had been an impulsive gesture, one that he should not have given in to. She'd had him wrapped around her little finger once before, then walked out on him. The last thing he needed was for her to realize how easy it would be for her to accomplish it again. He did not want her to see the extremely vulnerable spot that still existed inside him where Victoria Dalton Bingham was concerned.

He finally gave up trying to work, left the house and strolled down the path toward the stables. Maybe a hard ride through the hills would settle the nervous tension churning inside him.

Fred Olson looked up from his desk when Wyatt entered the tack room, a quizzical expression covering his face. "Afternoon, Wyatt. Somethin' I can do for ya?"

"Didn't mean to interrupt you, Fred. I thought I'd take one of the horses out for a ride."

"Need any help saddlin' up?"

"I can handle it, thanks." Wyatt grabbed a saddle, blanket and bridle and left the tack room.

It was just the type of afternoon for a brisk ride. The sky was blue, the sun just warm enough to take the coolness from the air without removing the crispness. He urged his horse into a trot as he cut across a field toward the stand of trees that marked the edge of the old trail he had enjoyed so much as a young man. Just as he emerged from the trees to join the trail, something flashed around a corner, startling his horse.

The animal reared, throwing Wyatt off his back, and the dirt bike and its rider skidded into a ditch. A moment later a teenage boy ran toward Wyatt as he lay on the ground.

"Are you okay, mister?"

Wyatt slowly got to his feet, testing his left leg before putting his full weight on it. He brushed the dirt from his jeans. "Yes, I seem to be all right. How about you?"

"Yeah." The teenager glanced back over his shoulder. "But I don't know about my bike."

Wyatt grabbed the reins of his horse, then walked toward the ditch. "Well, let's take a look at it and see."

The boy set the bike upright and Wyatt bent down to check the frame and wheels. A couple of minutes later he stood up. "It seems to be okay, except for some scratches in the paint. Hop on it and see if it rides the way it should."

Wyatt watched as the young man rode about fifty feet down the trail and then back again. "How does it handle?"

"Handles okay," the boy replied.

"You do know you're trespassing on private property—" he saw the objection form on the boy's face and his posture take on a defensive stance "—although the signs seem to have disappeared and I saw where the fence needs replacing."

He scrutinized the teenage boy for a moment. "So, what are you doing out here zipping around a horse trail on a dirt bike? Do you live somewhere nearby?" he asked. neither angry nor accusatory, merely curious.

"Yeah, I live in town. Me and my friend Tim were riding on this trail the other day. I didn't know this was someone's property. I guess Tim didn't know it either."

Wyatt placed his foot in the stirrup and swung up

on his horse. He looked down at the teenage boy, taking a moment to study him before speaking. "Try to be more careful from now on, okay?"

"Sure thing, mister." The boy got back on his bike and rode in the direction of town.

Wyatt watched as the boy disappeared around the curve in the trail. Something about him touched Wyatt, something that seemed familiar, but he did not know what it was or why. The disturbing feeling continued to nag at him as he rode back to his house.

Richie arrived home just as Vicki returned from work. He did not move fast enough to hide the results of his mischief from her scrutiny.

"What happened here, Richie? How did you rip your shirt and what happened to your bike?"

"It's nothing, Mom. I was riding in the hills and some guy came out of the woods on a horse. He got thrown off and I skidded into a ditch. That's all. It was no big deal."

"No big deal? Someone could have been seriously injured. Who was this man?"

"I don't know, just some guy on a horse."

"He didn't tell you his name?"

The irritation sounded in Richie's voice. "I don't know who he was. He didn't get hurt. I didn't get hurt. The horse didn't get hurt. My bike only got a couple of scratches. That's all there was to it."

"What, uh…" The nervous jitter started in the pit of her stomach. "What did this man look like?"

"I don't know. He was just some guy. I never saw him before. He was tall with dark hair. He was older, even older than you are."

Richie leveled a curious look at her, followed by a

withering sigh that said he was sure her advanced age had affected her reasoning. "So what's the big deal?"

"It's nothing. I just thought he might have been someone I knew." She tried to put forth a smile that said it was unimportant, but she was not sure how successful she was. "Why don't you go on in and clean up while I start dinner?"

She went through the motions, but her mind was not on preparing the meal. All the land back in the hills belonged to the Edwards family—or, more accurately, Wyatt Edwards. Could he possibly be the man whom Richie had run into?

She closed her eyes and took a calming breath. She knew there was no way to keep Wyatt from coming in contact with her son in such a small town, but she certainly had not intended for them to meet when she was not there to control what happened. How was it possible for everything to be falling apart like this? She felt a tear trickle down her cheek.

"Are you okay, Mom?"

She looked up to find Richie standing in the kitchen door, staring at her. She could not quite read the expression on his face, but he looked concerned.

"No one got hurt and I'm sorry about ripping my shirt. It really was an accident, Mom. Honest."

She breathed a sigh of relief, his words telling her that his concern emanated from an entirely different place than hers. But she knew the relief was only temporary. She would be seeing Wyatt again; there was no way of avoiding it. She also knew that each confrontation would bring her one step closer to what she feared the most.

Three

"I'm going to my dental appointment. I should be back in about an hour and a half, if that's all right." Noreen grabbed her purse from beneath the counter.

"That's fine. I have some paperwork to catch up on. Things seem to be pretty slow right now. In fact, they've been quiet all morning." Vicki watched as Noreen left the store, then she returned to the order she had been working on for the grocery distributor.

Wyatt peered through the doorway separating the post office from the market. As soon as Noreen exited through the front door, he entered through the back.

"Good morning." He tried to sound cheerful even though that was not the way he felt. The impulsive embrace of the previous day kept running through his mind. Even though it rekindled the passionate feelings he had been carrying inside him, it also reinforced the anger and hurt. There was a lot to reconcile, a lot she had to answer for.

Vicki locked up from her paperwork. "Uh...good morning." She refused to allow any hint of the warmth his touch had caused to show in her expression. She did not want him to think she was happy to see him again, especially after the way he had pulled her into his arms.

Wyatt proceeded directly to the counter, his attitude all business. "I would like to place an order for some special food items. Can you handle that or do I need to go to the city to procure what I want?"

"If my distributor handles the items, then I will be able to get them for you. I'm just putting together an order now." She looked up at him, trying her best to maintain a professional manner. "What is it you want?"

"What is it I want?"

She saw the slightly wicked grin tug at the corners of his mouth and the glow in his eyes. An edge of irritation crept into her voice as she tried to ignore his innuendo. "What items would you like me to order for you?"

He reached into his pocket and withdrew a piece of paper. "I've written them down." He slid the list across the counter toward her.

She reached for it, but he refused to release it from his grasp. She tugged at the piece of paper, then shot him a questioning look. "Are you going to let me see your list, or not?"

He was not ready to let her off the hook yet. He fully intended to toy with her a little longer. One way or the other he would get some answers from her. "Just as soon as you agree to sit down and have a

serious discussion about some unsettled matters.
Maybe we could talk over lunch.'' He leveled an even
gaze at her, turned on his best smile and waited for
her response.

She quickly withdrew her hand. ''I can't possibly
leave. Noreen is gone. By the time she gets back, it'll
be too late—''

''Too late for what? Too late to talk over lunch?
Then how about dinner? We could go into the city
and—''

''No, I...uh...I can't have dinner with you. I...I
have other plans.'' How was she ever going to exist
in the same small community as Wyatt Edwards? Why
was he doing this to her? Why was he being so per-
sistent? He had walked out on her—actually, he had
run out on her—and she did not understand why he
now apparently wanted to pick up the pieces of the
old relationship.

''You have other plans? But I haven't even sug-
gested a specific night for dinner. How could you possibly know that you have plans?'' Wyatt noted the
nervous way she avoided any eye contact with him,
the way she kept biting at her lower lip. He *needed* to
know what it was about him that made her so uncomfortable after all these years. It had to be more than
lingering guilt over her decision to run off and get
married while he was away on business. That decision
had apparently been easy enough for her to make fifteen years ago, he thought bitterly. There was no reason for it to be bothering her now.

She ran her fingers through her hair as she glanced
out the window. ''I assumed you meant tonight.''

''I did, but as luck would have it, my entire week

is open. Why don't you tell me which night you don't have plans?''

She bit at her lip again, the panic welling inside her faster than she could push it down. "I'm busy every night."

"Every night?'' he challenged. "I didn't think there was that much to do in this little town. Tell me, is there some sort of list of events? What's happening— a barn raising, a square dance, an ice-cream social? Is it rodeo season? Or perhaps big-city culture has come to Sea Cliff in the form of a new art gallery opening, a stage production of some sort, or maybe a live concert. Where do I find a list of these community activities so that I can participate, too?''

"No, it's not that. I'm just busy, that's all." She felt light-headed, as if all the oxygen had been sucked from the air. He was so near and so damnably sexy. But even if it was not a matter of protecting her son, she knew she could never succumb to his charm again. She was certain that over the past fifteen years he had left a string of broken hearts in his wake…hearts just like hers. She knew she could not bear the pain of having him walk away from her a second time.

"Okay, let's try it this way." He grabbed her calendar from next to the cash register. "Now, you can't have lunch with me today because your clerk won't be back until later this afternoon. Okay, that sounds reasonable."

He took her pen from the counter and wrote *no lunch* on the calendar. "Now, as for dinner tonight…you claim you're busy." He looked up, capturing her with his gaze. "Busy doing what? Is this the night you wash your hair?'' He reached out and touched her ash-blond hair, then allowed his fingertips to skim across her jaw and finally come to rest under her chin.

His voice took on a soft quality, betraying the emotion he was trying to conceal. "Your hair looks lovely. So do you."

Her entire body trembled beneath his touch. All she could think of was where the embrace they had shared might have led if she had not pulled away from him. She worried about him trying it again. She knew she would be powerless to stop it.

"Wyatt...I...I have work to do..." she finally managed to say. She closed her eyes and turned her head away. "Please go." Her voice was a mere whisper.

As much as he wanted to continue the seduction that seemed to have materialized of its own volition, he recognized that any further conversation along those lines would be counterproductive. He returned to the business at hand. "What about my order? Will you be able to get the items for me?"

"I'll call you after I've talked to my distributor."

"Fair enough." He wrote his phone number on her calendar. "I'll talk to you later."

Vicki breathed a sigh of relief when he walked out the door. Maybe the thing to do would be to have lunch with him, in some brightly lit public place, and put an end to things once and for all. She would tell him she was not interested in him, and to confine their unavoidable conversations to strictly business matters.

Speaking of business, she picked up his list and glanced at the items he wanted her to order. She swallowed hard and forced down the now familiar jittery feeling. Every item on his list was something that had been one of her favorites, things he would pick up for her whenever he went into the city.

Why was he doing this to her? He had coldly walked out on her. What could he possibly hope to gain by this sudden pretense of wanting to get back together? Was it all some sort of game for him, just as it had apparently been fifteen years ago? She shook her head in a determined manner. It did not matter. At least that was what she tried to tell herself. She would place his order. It would be a straightforward business transaction—nothing more.

She reached for the phone and dialed her grocery distributor. "Sam, I have a special order here. Do you carry these items?"

Vicki locked up the market and went to her office in the back room of the post office. She had some paperwork to take care of before going home. She sat at the desk, turned on the lamp, and took the journal from the drawer.

"The front door was locked, but I saw the light and figured you were in the office."

Wyatt's voice startled her. She had not heard anyone come in through the post office. She was not sure quite what to say. "We're closed for the day. Unless you're just checking your post-office box for mail, I'm afraid you'll have to come back some other time."

"I've already checked my mail." He walked into the office and sat on the edge of her desk, making himself at home without being invited.

Vicki leaned back in her chair in an attempt to put a little more distance between her and this man's very unsettling nearness. "Are you here about your special order? I talked to my distributor and all of your items will be here day after tomorrow. They usually deliver by ten o'clock in the morning, so anytime after that—''

He grabbed her hand and pulled her up from the chair. ''That's not why I'm here. I thought we could continue our discussion about your busy schedule. You claimed to be very busy tonight, so how about lunch tomorrow?''

Vicki worked her hand loose from his grasp and walked across the office. She bit at her lower lip as she turned things over in her mind. Finally she turned around to face him. ''If I have lunch with you this one time, will you stop pestering me?''

Wyatt slid off the edge of her desk, cocked his head, then took a couple of steps in her direction. ''Pestering you? I didn't realize being invited to lunch was so bothersome for you. After all, we're old friends. I thought we had lots to talk about, all kinds of things to catch up on.''

His tone and attitude spoke louder than his voice and she did not like them. He was making it very clear that he wanted to dredge up the past, and she still could not imagine why.

Then a new fear hit her. Perhaps he had found out about Richie.

Wyatt did not wait for a response. Once more, against his better judgment he pulled her into his arms. Before she could squirm out of his embrace, he captured her mouth with a kiss that at first was tentative, but quickly became demanding. Suddenly the past was very much alive. And all the old feelings came rushing back with a vengeance.

He had to know what happened between them, why she had walked away. How could something he thought was so perfect—still seemed so perfect—have fallen so completely apart without a single warning sign? He wanted the answers. He had dated other women—lots of other women. He had even managed to become engaged for a few months before he broke it off. But no one had ever replaced Vicki in his heart. He had to know what went wrong the first time—what had caused her to leave.

Wyatt had done it to her again. Vicki found herself completely under the spell of his magnetic sex appeal, combined with her very real feelings for him, even after all these years. As much as she intellectually *knew* that she had to break off the kiss and make him leave, she could not bring herself to do it. Somehow her arms ended up around his neck and her fingers threaded through his thick hair.

The kiss exploded with all the passion they had shared fifteen years ago. Wyatt skillfully maneuvered her toward the office couch, only a couple of steps away. A moment later they were half seated and half reclining...and fully entangled in each other's embrace.

He pulled her body tightly against his. Everything about her excited him more than he had anticipated and even more than his memory of their last time together. The silky quality of her hair, the creamy texture of her skin—it was all so familiar yet at the same time enticingly new. He did not know about the practicality of them making love on the couch in her office, but practical matters were rapidly being shoved to the farthest corner of his consciousness. He slipped his tongue between her lips, reveling in the taste that he had once known so intimately.

Vicki's mind reeled with confusion. Her logic tried to tell her to keep her distance from him, but her long-

denied physical desires soared from the heady reality
of his kiss. It was the type of kiss that could only lead
to one thing and it was an eventuality that she had to
prevent at all costs. Summoning up all her remaining
inner strength, she managed to pull back from him
enough to break the kiss.

"This…this is no good, Wyatt."

"It feels pretty good to me," he said, his words
thick with his excitement.

"It has to stop right now." She pushed away as she
attempted to calm her labored breathing.

He drew in a ragged breath. "Why?"

Why? How could he even ask such a question? He
had hurt her beyond words when he had so callously
deserted her. She was not going to play that game with
him again. Besides, the more practical matter of here
and now was that she had a son at home, a son who
would come looking for her if she did not show up
soon. The last thing she wanted or needed was for
Richie to catch her in a heated embrace with this man.

She struggled to extricate herself. "I need to get
home. I…I have several things to do yet tonight."

He straightened, allowing her to move away from
him while still holding onto her hand. "Like what?"

Vicki rose to her feet, freeing her hand from his
grasp. She stepped away from the couch, then ruffled
her fingers through her short hair in an effort to
smooth it away from her face. She could feel the flush
of embarrassment spread across her cheeks—embarrassment combined with panic over where her unre-
solved feelings for Wyatt had almost taken her.

Her voice was barely above a whisper. "Personal
things."

"Anything I can help you with?"

She shook her head, unable to force out any more words. She desperately needed to get away from the all-too-powerful presence of Wyatt Edwards. It had been way too easy for him to initiate an intimate situation, smoothly getting past all her defenses. And it felt far too comfortable being back in his arms again. What had almost happened between them frightened her to her very core.

He started toward her. "Can I at least walk you home?"

"No." She had blurted out her answer too quickly to a question that had not been asked in a hostile manner. She took a calming breath and tried again. "No...thank you. It's not necessary. It's only one block."

He brought her hand to his lips and started to pull her into his embrace once again, but she quickly stepped out of his reach.

"Please, Wyatt...let's not repeat that mistake." She knew she would not be able to muster the inner strength needed to break it off a second time.

"Mistake?" He cocked his head and raised an eyebrow. "What mistake is that?"

She ran her hand across her nape in an attempt to still the tremor of anxiety that coursed through her. Summoning up as much resolve as she could, she spoke in a very deliberate manner. "Don't play games with me. That little scene on the couch...it never should have happened. You know that and I know that."

"I don't know any such thing." He could not figure out what was happening between them. He was the one who had been wronged. She had walked out on him and married another man. For some reason he could not quite grasp, she acted far more nervous than guilty. It was a very puzzling situation. Whatever the problem, it apparently was not going to be resolved that night.

He reached out for her hand. "Are we on for lunch tomorrow?"

"I…" The intensity in his eyes was more than she could handle. She quickly averted her gaze. "I guess so."

"Good night, Vicki. I'll see you tomorrow."

She watched as Wyatt left the office. She heard the outside door open and close, and continued to listen as a car engine came to life, the noise receding as the automobile continued down the street.

Vicki collapsed onto the couch. A new concern penetrated her confusion. It was one she had thought she would never have to deal with, but now that she had come face-to-face with Wyatt again she feared she could not avoid it any longer. Did she have the right to deny Wyatt his son? It had been an easy question to answer when he had not been present in her life. But that was no longer the case. Even though he was not technically a part of her life again, she certainly had to admit there was no way to avoid him.

Whose best interest took priority and whose rights were more important—her son's or Wyatt's? It would be a much easier question to deal with if her son did not already believe someone else was his father—a kind and loving man who had provided them with a secure and happy home, then had suddenly been taken away, leaving a horrible vacancy. Did she have the right—or even the obligation—to take Richie's memory of that man and change it forever? She did not know the answer, but she did know the question was tearing her apart.

The following morning proved to be a busy one for Vicki and Noreen. Before Vicki was ready for it, the clock showed eleven forty-five. Wyatt would be arriving any minute for their lunch date. No, it was simply two people sharing a simple noontime meal—nothing more. Hardly a *date*. Definitely *not* a date.

She did not have much time for her speculations. A couple of minutes later Wyatt strolled casually through the front door of the store. He offered a pleasant smile, as if the passion of the previous night had never happened. "Are you ready for lunch?"

She looked around, raking her gaze over the store in an effort to make sure things were under control. "Yes, I guess I'm ready," she said, a noticeable lack of enthusiasm in her voice. She gathered her purse from beneath the counter and turned toward Noreen. "I won't be gone very long." Her words were more for Wyatt's benefit than anything else.

Wyatt escorted her to his car.

"I made a lunch reservation at the Harbor Inn. I hope the food there is still as good as it used to be. Of course, the view will help make up for any flaws in the cuisine." He shot her a quick glance as they drove down the highway. "Have you eaten there since your return to Sea Cliff?"

It was an innocent enough question on the surface, but the implications ran much deeper. It was where Wyatt had taken her for dinner the night after they had made love on the beach. It had been an intimate evening, complete with a promise for the future—a future that never happened.

"No. Things have been very hectic for me since I returned. I haven't had an opportunity to eat out at all."

"Well, I guess I'll have to rectify that." Outwardly Wyatt was upbeat and cheerful, all the while hiding the uneasiness that churned inside him. Even though Vicki seemed to have relaxed somewhat since they left her store, he could still feel the tension that seemed to fill the car as they drove down the road. It was almost as if she was frightened of something. It made no sense to him, no sense at all. What could she be hiding?

As they drove the twenty miles to the city, he made a continual effort to engage in light conversation and finally Vicki began to relax, slowly succumbing to his open, charming manner.

When they arrived at the Harbor Inn, they were seated in a quiet corner overlooking the ocean. As soon as they had ordered lunch and the waitress had removed their menus, he reached across the table to take her hand. While she did not jerk her hand away, she did remove it quickly from his reach.

"So, what have you been up to for the last fifteen years? You got married and now you're a widow. That's pretty much all I know."

She nervously glanced around the restaurant. "There's really not much to tell." She had made a horrible mistake when she agreed to have lunch with him. She'd thought they would go to a coffee shop and grab something to eat, then she would go back to work. She had not counted on any of this. She continued to look around the restaurant, trying her best to keep the memories from flooding her mind. There did not seem to be any escape. She was twenty miles from home and they had come in his car.

"Okay, maybe it will break through this wall you seem to have constructed between us if I tell you what I've been doing. Apart from a brief stay in South America, I spent most of my time in Europe, working out of our London office, until ten years ago when Dad passed away. The experience abroad was once-in-a-lifetime, and I loved it."

The stab of pain cut deep inside her. It was just as his father had told her that horrible day so many years ago. He had left the country in an attempt to get away from her. Even hearing it directly from Wyatt's mouth did not make it any easier for her to understand why he felt such a desperate need to get away from her...or why he insisted on telling her about it now.

Wyatt continued, seemingly unaware of the effect his words had on her. She did notice that his expression had become hard and a cynical edge tinged his words.

"Then ten years ago I took over the San Francisco corporate headquarters and have been there since. I had barely settled in when I found myself embroiled in a battle for control of the company. It seems that some of the executive staff felt that at twenty-seven years of age I was too young to be running the business. They quickly learned exactly where things stood." His voice softened and he became somewhat reflective. "That sure toughened me up in a hurry...taught me that I had to fight for what I wanted."

"What was it you wanted?" The question popped out of her mouth before she could stop it. She felt the flush of embarrassment spread across her cheeks. The intense darkening of his blue eyes forced her to look away. Then she felt his hand cover hers.

"What did I want? Pretty much what I still want— what I've always wanted."

She trembled beneath his touch, and quickly withdrew her hand as anxiety welled inside her. Was this just another game on his part? Renewed interest in having another fling that could only end in disaster when he grew tired of her and walked out again, just as he had before? She could not afford to pursue the answers to those questions. She had her son to take care of and he had to come before any personal considerations.

At that moment the waitress brought their food, providing a welcome break from the tension that had grown almost unbearable for Vicki. She forced an upbeat manner and offered an attempt at a smile. "This looks good." She made a tentative stab at her chef's salad with her fork, then reached for the breadbasket. "I didn't realize I was so hungry until I smelled the aroma of fresh-baked rolls."

She kept up a line of light, unimportant chitchat all during lunch. She did not want to allow Wyatt to take control of the conversation and turn it into a discussion of ancient history. Too many bad memories had already been dredged up. She did not want to discuss them, and certainly not with the man who had wounded her so deeply. All she wanted at that moment was for lunch to be over. "I really must be getting back to the store. I've been gone much too long as it is." She picked up her purse and prepared to leave.

"Vicki..." He reached out for her arm, preventing her from standing up. "We need to talk."

She once again disengaged from his touch before it

totally melted her resolve. "I thought we had just spent—" she glanced at her watch "—an hour and a half talking. Lunch was very nice, but now I must get back to work. Noreen has been there all by herself and I'm sure she could use a break." She quickly stood, signaling that she felt the conversation was at an end and it was time to leave.

"You know as well as I do that we have things to talk about."

Why was he doing this to her? Why did he insist on hurling the reality of his desertion into her face? "We have nothing to talk about," she snapped. "Now, I need to get back to the store. I've been gone too long."

Wyatt reluctantly rose from his chair, making no effort to hide his displeasure at the turn of events. He was not sure how to proceed. Every time he tried to broach the subject of their past, she became angry and defensive. For some reason that he had not yet been able to figure out, the topic seemed to make her very nervous. If running the family business had taught him nothing else, it had taught him perseverance. One way or another they would clear the air. He would get his answers.

The drive back to Sea Cliff turned into a very tense twenty miles. He occasionally glanced in Vicki's direction and said something, but she refused to acknowledge his attempts at conversation. She simply stared straight ahead. He saw no indication in her expression of what was going on in her mind. It had him perplexed, exasperated...and angry. He was trying to resolve the pain he still carried with him. And to do that, he needed to know what had prompted her irrational behavior of fifteen years ago.

Wyatt pulled up in front of the market. She immediately opened the door and slid out of the car before he could turn off the engine. She would not participate in his little game a second time. She would not put her emotions on the line again. Her voice carried the stress that churned inside her. "Thank you for lunch. It was...uh...nice seeing you again." Then she hurried inside the store without looking back.

Wyatt sat in stunned silence as he watched Vicki disappear into the market. He had found her earlier behavior odd, but it was nothing compared to the bizarre actions he had just witnessed. He did not know whether to be angry or concerned.

He thought for a moment, then climbed out of his car. He clenched his jaw in determination as he marched into the store, heading straight to the counter. He grabbed her arm, totally ignoring Noreen, with whom she had been engaged in conversation.

"We're going to talk right now!" It was an emphatic statement that left no room for disagreement. Before she could even attempt any type of rebuttal, he marched toward the back office with her in tow.

Vicki had trouble keeping up with his fast pace. Her initial anxiety quickly turned to anger as he nearly dragged her into the office and closed the door. Only then did he let go of her arm.

Her furious words matched her outraged expression. "How dare you do that to me! How dare you walk into my place of business and manhandle me like that!"

His anger equaled hers. "This has gone on long enough. I've tried to be nice, and Lord knows I've been extremely patient. But none of it has done any good. All my efforts have met with resistance from you, and some of them have even been met with rudeness. I want to know why." He fixed her with a hard look meant to intimidate her at the very least. "I want some answers, Vicki. I want some answers and I want them right now!"

She glared at him, refusing to back down. "You have no right to come in here ranting and raving, issuing ultimatums and ordering me around—absolutely no right at all. Now leave my office at once!"

"No right?" He grabbed her arm again. "Fifteen years ago—"

She jerked her arm from his grasp and took a step backward. "That's ancient history. I don't want to talk about what happened fifteen years ago!"

How dare he! He had walked out on her and now, fifteen years later, he wanted to sit down and casually discuss it as if it was no more important than choosing a restaurant for dinner.

"Well, we're going to talk about it, and we're going to talk about it right now." Even though he pushed to maintain a forceful attitude, he had been taken aback by her adamant refusal to talk about the past. Well, he could be just as stubborn as she was. "I want this settled once and for all."

"Hey, Mom...you back here?" Richie's voice became louder as he drew nearer. "Why is the door closed?"

Total panic shot through her, spreading to every corner of her existence. Her heart pounded so hard she feared it would burst out of her chest. Her gaze darted from Wyatt to the closed office door, then back to Wyatt. She saw his eyes widen in shock as he looked in the direction of the voice.

The moment she had feared most was at hand and

there was no way for her to stop it. She stood frozen
to the spot, watching the door open as if it was happening in a dream.

Or her very worst nightmare.

Four

"Mom?" Richie charged through the door, then came to an abrupt halt when he spotted Wyatt. He looked at him, then returned his attention to his mother.

"Is something wrong, Mom?" Richie became immediately protective, jumping into the role he had assigned to himself upon Robert Bingham's death—that of man of the house. "What's going on here?" His curiosity turned to suspicion as he stared pointedly at Wyatt.

"It's nothing, Richie. We were just discussing… uh…a special order that Mr. Edwards had placed." Her insides churned. It took all her ability to still the quaver in her voice.

Richie eyed her skeptically, then glanced at Wyatt again.

Wyatt had finally managed to recover from the

shock. He tried to force a calm demeanor as he spoke to the teenage boy standing before him. "Well...so you're Richie? You never mentioned that you were Vicki's son."

Wyatt shot a pointed look in Vicki's direction. "And *you* never mentioned that you *had* a son."

Richie turned toward his mother. "This is the guy I ran into back in the hills."

"Uh...yes...I suspected as much. Richie, this is Wyatt Edwards. He owns all of that land, including the large house up on the hill."

Richie immediately stuck out his hand and projected his most grown-up manner. "It's nice to meet you...officially."

"It's nice to meet you, too." Wyatt accepted Richie's handshake, then glanced in Vicki's direction again just in time to see her biting at her lower lip. There was no mistaking her nervousness, nor the very real fear in her eyes.

She quickly put her arm around her son's shoulder. "Shouldn't you be home doing your schoolwork?" She tried her best to ease him toward the office door without appearing obvious.

Richie furrowed his brow in confusion. "Don't you even want to know why I'm home from school early?"

"Yes, of course I do. I just thought we could talk about it at dinner." She chuckled nervously. "I'm sure it's nothing that would be of interest to Wyatt."

Richie's gaze darted from his mother to Wyatt and back to his mother again. "Sure, Mom," he said cautiously, a confused expression on his face. He stole another quick sideways glance at Wyatt. "Are you sure everything is okay here?"

She gave him a confident smile. "Of course it is. Now you run along home and do your schoolwork and I'll be there in a couple of hours."

Vicki watched as Richie left the office. She dared not look in Wyatt's direction. She knew the physical resemblance between her son and his biological father would be too much for her to handle at that moment. She silently prayed that she was the only one who noticed it.

"Why didn't you mention you had a son?" Wyatt spoke in a very controlled manner, carefully measuring each and every word.

His question cut through her like a hot knife through butter. The mixture of incredulity and borderline outrage in his voice made her feel very uncomfortable. She refused to look at him. "I...uh...I guess it never came up in conversation."

"Oh, I see." He crossed the room toward her. He made no attempt to squelch the sarcasm in his voice. "Just a little thing that sort of slipped your mind?" An overwhelming sadness settled over him, and he experienced a tremendous sense of loss. Richie should have been *their* son.

Vicki did not acknowledge his comments. She turned toward the office door. "I have to get back to work. There's lots to do before closing time."

He caught her arm and brought her to a halt. "We have to talk about this, Vicki. We have to get everything out in the open."

She jerked her arm out of his grasp. "What happened fifteen years ago is in the past. Dredging it all up again serves no purpose." He had walked out on her, he had hurt her. She had no interest in reliving it. "Why can't you just leave it alone?" she snapped.

"Until we've settled the past, we can't deal with the present…or the future."

"We have no present…." She fought back the tears of despair. "Nor can there be any future." Her words came out as a barely audible whisper and then she hurried out of the office without looking at him.

Wyatt leaned back against her desk and watched her walk away from him, just as she had walked away from him so long ago. Once again, he did not know why. The only difference was that this time he knew where to find her.

He thought about Richie and recalled the look of fear on Vicki's face when her son had called out to her. It left him with a very unsettled feeling that he could not categorize. He heaved a sigh, then forced himself to move. He got in his car, and drove home.

Vicki finished out the afternoon and went home to prepare dinner. As soon as she entered the kitchen, she knew she was in for trouble. Richie looked up from his books and the expression on his face said he, too, was looking to her for some answers.

She forced an upbeat manner. "How's the home-work coming?"

"I'm done." As if to add emphasis to his words, he closed his book and set it aside.

She busied herself by taking things from the refrigerator and from the cupboards and setting them on the counter.

"Mom—"

"I'll have dinner ready in just a bit. I imagine you're starved."

His tone of voice became more emphatic. "Mom—"

"So...why were you home from school early?" She did not want to hear what she knew he was going to say.

His words came out in an exasperated rush. "There was a power failure at school—no electricity. They sent everyone home early."

He quickly followed up with what he wanted for dinner before Vicki had an opportunity to interrupt him again. Then he said, "What were you and that Wyatt guy arguing about? Is he someone you knew from before?"

This was just about the last conversation she wanted to have with her son, but there did not seem to be any way of avoiding it. She forced a smile. "We weren't arguing. I told you, he had placed an order for some special items and we were discussing it. That's all." She reached out to smooth his hair away from his face.

He stepped out of her reach while flashing a look of irritation. "Cut it out, Mom." He eyed her suspiciously. "I don't buy your story."

Vicki adopted her official mother attitude. "Well, young man, it doesn't matter whether you buy it or not. That's the way it is and there's no more to say about it."

His expression showed a hint of defiance as he continued to stare at her. Finally he turned to pick up his schoolbooks. "Yeah...right." His tone of voice told her he did not believe a word she'd said.

She watched as he left the kitchen and headed for his bedroom. She could not chastise him for his disrespectful attitude when he had been correct. Her boy was growing up. He was a young man now and as such had elected to act as her protector against what he perceived as a threat.

Things were becoming very difficult. How could she protect a boy who stood on the brink of adulthood and tried so hard to be the man of the family? She could not forbid him to talk to Wyatt. In fact, any attempt on her part to steer him away from contact with Wyatt would only result in questions she was not prepared to answer.

She closed her eyes for a moment in an attempt to force some sort of insight to appear, some flash of brilliance to make itself known. Unfortunately nothing materialized.

Wyatt's car screeched to a halt in the circular drive in front of his house. He slammed the front door behind him, then took the staircase two steps at a time. He went directly to his private suite, grabbed a bottle of beer from the mini-refrigerator in his study, then plopped down on the couch.

It had all started as a simple idea—move back to the family house and run the business affairs from there, venturing to San Francisco only a few days each month. With fax machines and computers he had instantaneous access to those he needed to communicate with, including on-line visual conferencing.

But while the idea appeared simple enough on the surface, the underlying motivations were not as clear-cut. Wyatt was searching for something. At thirty-seven years of age he had certainly achieved notable recognition in the business world by steering the family corporation to even greater success than his father. He had acquired all the material possessions he needed.

But there still existed a gaping hole in his existence. It was a place that he had continued to hold available for Vicki in the hopes that one day they would reunite. It was that desire that had dictated his return to Sea Cliff, a desire to recapture the happier days of his past—when he and Vicki had been together.

Well, here they were. They had both returned to Sea Cliff and they were both single.

And Vicki had a son.

Vicki inventoried and logged in the delivery from her grocery distributor. Along with her regular order, the delivery included the items Wyatt had requested. She packed them into a box, then prepared an invoice for him. Pausing for a moment, she stared at the phone in the storage room. She shook her head. No, she would not call him. She had already told him his order would be in on Friday. She would leave it up to him to come and collect it today.

She joined Noreen in the market. Friday and Saturday were their busiest days of the week. The rest of the morning passed quickly with a continual stream of customers. Before Vicki realized how much time had elapsed it was almost four o'clock. Then she saw it— Wyatt's car pulling up to the curb in front of the market. The anxiety immediately started churning in the pit of her stomach. She suspected she would probably end up with an ulcer before this was through. A moment later Wyatt entered through the front door.

He walked directly to Vicki. "You didn't call. May I assume my order arrived as scheduled?" His tone did not contain any hint of his feelings about what had happened the day before.

"Yes…your order is here. I've been very busy and didn't have a chance to call." She avoided eye contact with him as she stepped out from behind the counter and started toward the storage room. "I'll get it for you."

Wyatt chose not to stand idly by and wait for her to return. He followed her through the store. As soon as they were in the storage room, he pushed the door shut and grabbed her firmly by the shoulders, turning her around to face him. He studied her expression, searching for any signs of what it was that had her so frightened.

He gradually loosened his grip on her without letting go, then pulled her to him and held her in his arms. He ran his fingers through her hair and cradled her head against his shoulder. If only he could figure out what was going on. Two days ago, her kiss had said all the passion still existed, yet now she turned a cold shoulder to him without any reason that he could understand. She behaved as if he had done something wrong.

"What's wrong, Vicki? What is it that has you so frightened?" he said softly.

She felt so safe and protected in his arms, just as she had so many years ago before everything fell apart—before he had broken her heart. "Nothing... nothing is frightening me." She knew the words had been uttered without conviction. Even to her own ear they sounded hollow.

"I don't believe you." He did not sound accusatory, just very honest.

"It doesn't matter whether or not you believe me." She had to be strong. She couldn't let on that she was keeping the truth from him. "My life doesn't revolve around whether or not you believe me. That's the way it is."

"Is someone harassing you? Threatening you? Is

that why you decided to move back to Sea Cliff to run the business rather than selling it? Did you come here to get away from someone? To hide? I can have my company attorney get involved. We can hire a private detective or go to the sheriff—''

"No—it's nothing like that!" His assumption so surprised her that she blurted out the words without considering the unspoken information they conveyed—the fact that there was something, but he had incorrectly guessed what it was. She certainly could not tell him why she was afraid, especially since he was the cause of that fear.

Her insides felt as if they were being ripped apart, torn between her responsibility to her son and the forbidden desire she felt for Wyatt Edwards. He caressed her shoulders, then ran his hand across her back. She tentatively wrapped her arms around his waist. It took all her resolve to keep from completely melting in his arms. They stood still for several seconds, wrapped in the comfort of each other's embrace.

Wyatt placed his fingertips beneath her chin and raised her face until he could see her eyes—the brown eyes with amber flecks, surrounded by the long dark lashes. He saw the wariness and the caution. He brushed his lips gently against hers. "Come to my house tonight." It was not phrased as a question, but neither was it a demand.

"I...I can't. Richie will be home..." Her words trailed off as she pulled away from his embrace.

"Vicki—"

"I have to get back to work. I...I'm sorry, Wyatt." She hurried out of the storage room and through the market.

Wyatt stood at the back of the market and watched

as she took over the checkout counter from Noreen. She continued to bite at her lower lip while ringing up a sale on the cash register. If her son was the reason she did not want to see him, then perhaps he could remedy the situation by suggesting that the three of them do something together.

Now that he was over the initial shock of finding out she had a son, he had to admit to a curiosity about the boy. He did not know exactly how old Richie was, but it seemed obvious that when Vicki left him she went directly to the arms of another man. She had to have become pregnant immediately.

The anger began to well inside him. Exactly who was this other man? Was he someone she knew before he went to South America? Where did she meet him?

For a long time he had blamed her for leaving, but lately he had shifted some of that blame to himself— wondering if he had done something to drive her away. Even after all these years, the pain still lived inside him—the pain and the confusion.

Wyatt's thoughts were interrupted by Richie's arrival from school. He hurried in the front door of the store and approached Vicki.

"Tim wants to know if I can sleep over at his house tonight. Is it okay with you?"

Vicki looked up. She immediately spotted Wyatt, who was obviously listening to the conversation. If she said yes, then she would have no excuse for not seeing him. But if she said no, then it could result in Wyatt and Richie spending time together if he took it upon himself to simply show up at her door. Neither situation appealed to her, but having Richie safely out of the way seemed the lesser of two evils.

"Are Tim's parents going to be there?" She continued to steal glances at Wyatt, trying to read his reaction.

"His mom's going to be there. His dad has some kind of lodge meeting that he goes to one Friday each month."

"Are you sure it's okay with his mother? Should I call her?"

"For crying out loud, Mom. I'm not ten years old. I'm almost—"

"Well, if you're sure it's okay with Tim's mother, then it's okay with me." The last thing she wanted was for Richie to blurt out his exact age in front of Wyatt. It also sealed her decision. The lesser of two evils was to take her chances being alone with Wyatt. It was better than having him around her son.

"Victoria, I thought I warned you about allowing your son to associate with that Timmy Forsythe."

Vicki whirled in the direction of Alice Thackery's voice. The woman must have come in while she was preoccupied with Richie. Then she noticed the look on Alice's face as her glance went from Richie to Wyatt and then back to Richie. Panic, fear, her worst nightmare...everything hit Vicki at once. If anyone in town would go out of the way to make a connection between her son and Wyatt Edwards, it would be Alice Thackery.

"Hey! Tim isn't—" Richie directed his angry words toward Alice, but he never got to finish his sentence.

"You run along, Richie. I'll see you in the morning." The knots of anxiety drew tighter and tighter inside Vicki's stomach as she did her best to hustle her son out the door, out of Alice Thackery's sight.

Vicki stole a quick glance at Wyatt, noting the odd expression on his face.

Richie glared at Alice, then headed toward the door. "Sure…see you in the morning, Mom."

A moment later Wyatt stepped between the two women. "Well, Alice, just who appointed you to be in charge of choosing everyone else's friends? I believe Vicki's quite capable of looking after her own son without your assistance."

Alice's brow furrowed in concentration as she pointedly stared at Wyatt, almost as if she was studying him. Finally she spoke. "I resent your attitude, young man. Carrying the Edwards name does not give you permission to rudely interfere where you are not welcome. Now…I have some shopping to do." With that she turned her back on both Wyatt and Vicki and checked her grocery list.

Vicki tried to remain calm as she glared at Wyatt. "I believe I'm also capable of looking after my own son without *your* assistance."

She had just suffered the worst ten minutes she had spent in many years, but she did not see any signs of recognition on Alice's face. There was no reason to suspect that Alice had spotted the physical resemblance between Wyatt and Richie. She also knew she was only kidding herself if she really believed any of that.

Vicki left Noreen to deal with Alice Thackery's purchases as she hurried to her office in the back of the post office. She did not know whether to be furious over what had happened or scared to death of what Alice might say or do. Anger won. She started to slam the office door, but Wyatt caught it in time.

She whirled around and glared in his direction as

she gestured wildly toward the front of the market. She made no attempt to hide her resentment and her rage. "What gives you the right to interfere in my business?"

A somewhat bewildered Wyatt tried to soothe her. "I only thought an impartial opinion might show Alice—"

"And just who the hell does that miserable old busybody think she is anyway? How dare she—"

"Don't let her get to you like that." His words were soft and comforting. So were his arms as he pulled her into his embrace. "She's a bitter woman whose only joy in life seems to be making other people miserable. Don't allow her to do this to you."

The anger remained in her tone, even though she had calmed down quite a bit. "I don't care if she attacks me, but I won't allow her to attack my son."

Wyatt continued to hold her, gently caressing her shoulders and back. His thoughts, however, wandered to the image of Alice staring intently at Richie, then at him, then at Richie again. He could not wipe her odd expression from his mind.

Vicki eased her way out of his embrace, bringing his attention back to the present. He reluctantly allowed her to go, all except her hand, which he continued to clasp in his. "It seems that you no longer have any responsibilities for this evening, so I don't see any reason why we can't spend it together." He felt her tremble, then she offered him a weak smile.

"I guess there isn't any reason after all."

She was far from enthusiastic, but she had agreed. It was a small step but he was pleased. "I'll let you get back to work for now." He brushed a soft kiss across her lips. "I'll see you at closing time."

Wyatt left through the post-office entrance, taking his box of special-order items with him. Vicki remained in the back until she saw Alice Thackery leave, then she went to the front counter. She stared out the window and watched as Alice walked down the sidewalk, then she turned to Noreen.

"Humph! That woman really infuriates me."

"Oh, she's not that bad. I know she gets on lots of people's nerves. You just have to discount most of what she says, try not to take her too seriously." Noreen became reflective. "It's really kind of sad. I think she's a very lonely woman."

"Maybe if she made an effort to be more pleasant, she wouldn't be so lonely."

What was left of the workday passed quickly. Vicki locked the front door after Noreen left, then put the Closed sign in the window. She'd retreated to her office to finish up the day's paperwork when Wyatt appeared at her door.

"Hi, how's it going?"

She looked up at the sound of his voice. "You startled me. Where did you come from?"

"I came in through the post-office entrance. Are you about through for the day?"

She gave him a weary sigh. "Almost."

He walked into the office and sat on the edge of her desk. "As long as we both have to eat and Richie is already taken care of, I thought we might have dinner at your house. I'll provide the food and wine, and I'll even help with the cooking. How does that sound?"

She felt a sinking feeling in the pit of her stomach. She had not anticipated this turn of events. She had thought they might go to a movie. The idea of being alone with him for an extended period of time in private was not her idea of a prudent way to spend the evening—especially in light of the perplexing way he kept trying to dredge up the past as if it were nothing more than impersonal conversation to pass the time.

Her most recent run-in with Alice Thackery had left her shaken and scared. She needed some sort of comfort. As much as she knew how wrong it would be, her natural inclination was to gravitate toward Wyatt for that comfort. The sensible thing would be to stay as far away from him as possible. She knew she was walking a dangerous line.

"I guess that sounds okay," she said tentatively, as if she were not really convinced of what she was saying.

He flashed a dazzling smile. "Good." He looked around the office. "Ready to go?"

"Just a couple more minutes."

Vicki completed her work, put away the files, and locked the office door. She secured the door connecting the post office to the market, and together they left by the post-office exit.

When they reached his car, Wyatt opened the door for her. "I have everything we need right here."

She hesitated for a moment as she peered at the cardboard box inside the car. This was obviously not a spur-of-the-moment idea. He had come prepared for them to have dinner at her house...alone. It was her last opportunity to change her mind, to send him home. She slid into the car and he closed the door. She had made her decision.

Once they were at her house he did his best to create a comfortable atmosphere, to ease her obvious nervousness. He was pure charm as he worked his way back into her good graces. By the time the dinner dishes had been cleared away, they had almost settled into the same feeling of closeness they once enjoyed many years ago.

Wyatt carried two glasses of wine into the living room and he and Vicki sat on the couch. He handed her one of the glasses, then turned off the lamp, leaving only the light from the front hallway to provide soft illumination. He held his glass up to propose a toast.

"Here's to what has been and what is yet to be." They each took a sip of wine.

His words settled over her like a soft caress, and her concern disappeared in a heartbeat when he took the glass from her hand and set it on the end table.

He wrapped her in his embrace and snuggled back into the corner of the couch, pulling her with him. "It's been a long time, Vicki. I've often wondered what happened to you, what you were doing...whether or not you were happy with the way your life turned out." He had been wondering a lot more than that, but her adamant refusal to discuss the past dictated that he proceed slowly.

It was not what she had been expecting and she was not sure how to respond. Was it his attempt at saying he should not have left her? That he regretted past decisions? "I was wondering the same thing about you. What you had done with your life...and whether you were content with the choices you had made."

The choices *he* had made? What an odd thing for her to say. He did not understand what she meant by that. The *choice* that had the greatest impact on his life had not been his at all—it had been hers. Her decision to leave Sea Cliff without even saying goodbye had been a very painful blow, one he still had not recovered from.

Any further thoughts were put on hold when he claimed her mouth with all the passion he had been carrying inside him for the past fifteen years. He ran his fingers through her hair, then traced the length of her body. He felt her breathing, felt her breasts pressing against his chest. He desperately needed to break through the wall she hid behind. But for now that would have to wait.

The taste of her mouth excited him every bit as much as it had back then, possibly even more. He twined his tongue with hers in a ritual of seduction, a prelude to what he hoped would be a night of passion with a woman who had occupied his thoughts as no one else ever had.

Vicki was not sure how things had gotten so out of hand so quickly. One minute he was offering a toast that had made her very uncomfortable, and the next minute they were wrapped around each other and he was driving her crazy with a raw sensuality that she had never been able to erase from her memory. She had her son to think about, and she had to protect him at all costs. She could not allow this to happen, but she did not know how to stop it.

His seduction was too smooth and her desires too heated. Everything vanished from her mind except the excitement he stirred deep inside her. She gave one last, fleeting thought to how difficult things would be in the cruel light of dawn if she and Wyatt made love. But then her physical desires overruled logic and she totally succumbed to his passion. She did not know what tomorrow would bring, but for now they had tonight.

Wyatt felt the tension drain from her body, as if she had finally decided to let go of the battle raging inside her. At that precise moment he knew for a fact that they would make love...for the second time in their lives.

The first time they had made love had been an impulsive action, the culmination of runaway hormones. She had been a virgin and he knew the entire experience had been far more enjoyable for him than for her. Even though it had certainly been by mutual consent, she had become frightened afterward and had chosen not to make love with him a second time that night.

Now he had been given a second chance and he was determined to make up for having failed to give her everything she needed fifteen years ago. He nibbled his way across her cheek, then whispered in her ear, "It's been a long time, Vicki. I can't begin to tell you how much I've missed you." He slipped one hand under her blouse and up her bare back, reveling in the satiny texture of her skin.

"Please...no words." She could not bear to hear him say how much he had missed her. Not when he was the one who had caused their separation in the first place. But at the moment there was neither anger nor animosity. There was only heated desire that needed to be satisfied—and the love she felt for him that had never died.

Five

Wyatt worked his free hand between their bodies and began unbuttoning Vicki's blouse. The excitement spread inside him as each button gave way, exposing more and more of her bare skin to his touch. His hardened arousal pressed against the front of his jeans. With the passage of time, his love for her had grown more intense and he wanted her even more than he had that night on the beach.

The last button of her blouse slipped through the buttonhole, and he shifted their positions on the couch so that he could smooth the garment away from her shoulders and down her arms. Her blouse fell to the floor next to the couch. He placed little kisses across her shoulder and along her collarbone before tracing the edge of her lacy bra cup with the tip of his tongue. Then he ran his finger underneath the bra strap and over her shoulder.

Her ragged breathing matched his. Every fiber of her being burned for him. She craved his touch, his kiss, the feel of his body pressed against hers. This was all so very wrong, but she wanted him too much to care. The first time they had made love had been an equal mixture of excitement and apprehension. The experience had not lived up to what she imagined it would be, but it had not been Wyatt's fault. He had been patient and gentle with her. She had allowed her uneasiness to rob her of the full pleasure of their one and only intimacy. She did not intend that to happen again.

She ran her hands beneath his pullover shirt, once again touching the hardness of his chest before circling her arms around him. She caressed his tautly muscled back, releasing him long enough to allow him to unhook and remove her bra. He dropped it on the floor on top of her blouse. Then he frantically yanked his own shirt over his head and threw it on the floor.

The cool air in the room was in stark contrast to the heated atmosphere surrounding them. The coolness teased her bare breasts, accentuating the warmth of his hand as he cupped the underside before seductively drawing her nipple into his mouth.

A soft moan escaped her lips. Tremors of delight coursed through her body. Things had gone too far. But she could not put a stop to what was happening, even if she had wanted to. If they were to have only this one night together, then she wanted it to be enough to last her a lifetime.

"Oh, Wyatt…I can't—"

He took control of her mouth, nibbling and teasing with his lips until she managed to break the contact.

"I can't—"

His breath came in ragged gasps. "You can't what?"

She finally abandoned all pretense of an objection. "I can't believe I'm about to make love with you again after all these years."

"But you are, aren't you." The words came out of his mouth more in the form of a statement than a question.

"Yes...I am."

Her head sank back against the arm of the couch. She closed her eyes and totally gave herself over to his tantalizing seduction. She felt his arousal pressing against her thigh. She shifted her weight until she had him securely nestled between her denim-clad thighs. She ran her fingers through his thick hair, then cradled the back of his head with one hand while tracing his spine with her other hand.

The blood surged hot and fast through his veins. His heart pounded. Vicki projected wholesomeness and refinement, yet at the same time she had a sensual earthiness that could easily drive any man to distraction.

He teased her puckered nipple with his tongue before moving to her other breast. He suckled gently at first, then with increased fervor. He could not get enough of her—the feel of the pebbled texture against his tongue, the way each intake of her breath forced the delicate treat more fully into his mouth. His hands skimmed up her rib cage to the outside of her breasts. He sighed deeply, showing his contentment and pleasure, then kissed the tender spot over her heart.

He continued to lavish kisses on her—her throat, each nipple, the underside of each breast—as he slowly and seductively worked his way down her body, pausing when he arrived at the waist of her jeans. His fingers trembled slightly as he unsnapped them, then slowly lowered the zipper.

Wyatt did not need to make any requests. He leaned back and Vicki instinctively lifted her hips. He tugged at her jeans, pulling them down her long legs and depositing them on the floor with the other clothes. He paused a moment to take in the vision of this nearly naked woman with mussed hair and sparkling eyes. His gaze traced every line and curve of her body. "You're even more beautiful now than you were all those years ago," he said huskily.

The sight of her black lace bikini panties sent an added thrill coursing through him. She was, without a doubt, the most desirable woman he had ever known.

He reached for the waist of his own jeans. Vicki placed her hands on top of his, preventing him from unbuttoning his Levi's. "Here…let me do that." Her voice conveyed a barely controlled sensuality that raised the surrounding temperature several degrees.

She sat up on the couch with Wyatt standing in front of her. Considering the fact that she had not been with anyone in the five years since Robert's death, her hands were surprisingly steady as she unfastened the top button and lowered the zipper. Tonight she would shut out the world and allow herself to be whatever she wanted without worrying about her many responsibilities. She would be daring, even brazen. Just for tonight, she would make totally uninhibited love with the one man who had truly set her soul on fire.

She leaned forward and placed a soft kiss on his stomach while easing his jeans over his hips and down to his ankles. He stepped out and kicked them aside. Then she began inching his briefs down until his fully aroused manhood sprang free. She flicked the tip of her tongue along the length of his hardness. When she felt him shudder and heard his sharp intake of breath, a hot wave of excitement washed through her and settled deep inside.

A wicked grin turned up the corners of his mouth. "You certainly didn't know that little trick fifteen years ago " Before she could respond, he grabbed her by the wrist and pulled her up from the couch. Holding her body tightly against his, he ran his hands down her bare back and inside her panties. He nuzzled the side of her neck, kissed the tender spot behind her ear, then whispered seductively, "Let's abandon this couch and find a bed."

She tickled her fingertips across his bare bottom. "My bedroom is the first one on the right." Wiggling out of his embrace, she took a couple of steps toward the hallway.

"Just a minute." He grabbed his jeans from the floor and reached inside the pocket, withdrawing several concom packets.

Vicki stared at them for a moment. The need for birth control had not entered her consciousness. She had almost lost Richie twice to miscarriage and the ninth month of her pregnancy had been spent in bed. The doctor told her she would not be able to have any more children. But safe sex was another matter, and one that had to be acknowledged. She grinned mischievously at him. "So, you seem to have anticipated the outcome of the evening. Do you plan to use all of those?"

His eyes burned a smoldering cobalt blue as he grabbed her hand. "As many of them as my stamina will allow." He led her down the hall toward the bedroom.

Wyatt dropped the condom packets on the nightstand. He leaned Vicki back across the bed, then snuggled his body between her legs. The incendiary passions of a moment earlier had been temporarily set aside for more practical matters, but it did not take long for the heat to again burst into full flame.

He traced his fingertip across the swell of her breast and teased her nipple with his tongue. His thick words clearly attested to his state of heightened arousal. "Vicki...I've wanted—"

Once again she placed her fingertips against his lips to still his words. She did not want to hear whatever he intended to say. She could not endure any false words of endearment born of momentary passion. His mouth found hers with a kiss that tasted of hot lust and carnal desire, yet also spoke of caring and warmth. She drew Wyatt to her, encouraging his seduction of her body and her senses. She closed her eyes and forced away the fears and resentment from her mind, concentrating solely on the pleasure.

He kissed each tautly puckered nipple, ran the tip of his tongue along the underside of each breast, then grabbed the elastic band at the top of her panties with his teeth. He tugged at the panties, each yank pulling them lower and lower on her hips.

Little tremors of delight flitted across the surface of her skin. She arched her back, raising her hips from the bed. Wyatt eased the panties down her legs and tossed them toward the chair in the corner. His breath tickled her abdomen, then warmed the downy softness nestled at the apex of her thighs. His kiss gently teased her femininity at first, then captured it with a demanding possessiveness that took control of every fragment of her reality.

A hard jolt of sensual pleasure ripped through her body. Then another and another. The pure, unbridled ecstasy of the moment totally engulfed her. "Wyatt..." The utterance was as much a gasp as a word. "Hold me..."

He rolled over on his back and pulled her on top of him. He cupped the roundness of her bottom and held her tightly against his body. "You are the most exquisite—"

His words were replaced by a growl that was a mixture of pleasure and raw desire. Her touch was neither tentative nor hesitant as she sensually stroked his hardened need in a seductive manner he knew was far too exciting for him to endure for very long. He fumbled on the nightstand until he found one of the packets, then quickly ripped it open and removed the contents.

Vicki wrapped her arms around Wyatt's neck and opened herself to his intimate probe of the depth of her womanhood. She eagerly accepted him inside her, closing around his hardness. She responded to his smooth stroke and tantalizing rhythm by moving with him as if they were separate parts of the same whole.

Once again the convulsions started deep inside her and enveloped her entire body. She clung tightly to him as every fiber of her existence melted into total surrender. Then she felt his body stiffen.

The sensations were too intense, the pleasure too great. He had reached the limit of his control. He gave one last, deep thrust, then shuddered as powerful spasms raced through his body. He gulped in a lungful of air, hoping to ease his labored breathing as the spasms began to subside. He held Vicki to him, wanting that precise moment in time to last forever.

They remained quiet in each other's arms, basking in the afterglow of their lovemaking. She rested her head against his chest, the steady rhythm of his strong heartbeat filling her with a sense of security and a feeling of comfort and contentment. He cupped her breast in the warmth of his hand and occasionally stroked her hair. For several minutes they savored the sensation of their bodies pressed together, bare skin resting against bare skin.

Wyatt leaned over and covered her mouth with his in a soft kiss. That was all it took. One spark ignited the smoldering embers and once again the long pent-up passion that existed between them exploded into a raging inferno.

His tongue meshed with hers, filling him with the taste of her excitement. He trailed kisses across her face, down her throat, and across her shoulder. He continued to explore with his lips and tongue until he found her nipple. He teased the hardened bud, then took it into his mouth. He skimmed his fingertips up her inner thigh until he reached the moist heat of her sex.

As she had before, Vicki surrendered herself totally to the thrill of Wyatt's expert lovemaking. She murmured her delight at his skillful ministrations. But her soft murmurings dissolved into an earthy moan when he slipped his finger between the folds of her femininity.

Vicki stared at the glowing numerals on the bedroom clock. It was five in the morning. Wyatt's body radiated a soft warmth as he slept next to her.

It had been quite a night. Never had she felt so totally satiated. She turned over and watched him for a moment and a hint of sadness touched her. Before long, dawn would clear away the shadows and return her life to the reality of here and now. And she knew that life could not include Wyatt Edwards. He had walked out on her once, breaking her heart. She would not allow him the opportunity to do it again.

Wyatt stirred awake and immediately reached out for her, drawing her into his embrace. His words were thick with sleep. "Good morning." He nuzzled the side of her neck, then kissed behind her ear. "Mmm...I think I'd like to have you for breakfast." He ran his hand along the curve of her hip, then up her inner thigh.

Anxiety jittered inside Vicki. They did not have time for any sweet murmurings or intimate play. She edged away from him and slid out of bed, then grabbed her robe from the closet. "You have to leave."

He sat up and ran his fingers through his tousled hair. "Right now? It's not even daylight yet," he teased, as if he considered her statement a joke of some sort. "Are you planning to send me out into the cold, cruel dawn without a nice breakfast to warm me?"

He reached out to her, but she stepped back to avoid his touch. "Right now, Wyatt. You have to leave before it gets light out. It's bad enough that your car has been parked at my house all night. I can't afford to have anyone see you leave here. And Richie...my son will be home before long. I certainly can't have him find you here."

He noted the way she bit at her lower lip, the same

lip he had tasted many hours ago. He also saw the nervousness that covered her features. He furrowed his brow in confusion. "I don't get it, Vicki. Are you shutting me out? What about last night? Didn't it mean anything?"

"Apparently you've forgotten what living in a small town is like. There's no such thing as something not being anyone else's business. There's no such thing as live and let live. Besides, my concern isn't me. It's Richie. He would never understand this—"

Wyatt climbed out of bed and grabbed her arm, then pulled her into his embrace. "You can tell him that I just arrived to take you to breakfast." He leaned forward to kiss her, but she averted her face.

"No...I can't do that. Richie is a very bright boy and he's very observant. There isn't much that gets past him. He'd notice that you're wearing the same clothes you had on yesterday. Besides, I have to sort the mail at the post office before I open the market for business. He knows I wouldn't have time to go out for breakfast."

Wyatt turned her face back toward him. He saw it in her eyes again, the same fear and trepidation he had seen there before. "I don't get it. Last night was incredible, but this morning—"

"Last night shouldn't have happened," she said, a sharp edge creeping into her voice. "Nothing can come of our having made love. It—" She looked away, unable to maintain eye contact with him. "It was just one of those things, a momentary lapse in good judgment, and now it's over." She felt the tears begin to dampen her eyes. She quickly blinked them away.

"Just one of those things?" His anger came through

in spite of his obvious effort to maintain a calm tone.
"Are you honestly trying to tell me that last night was
nothing more than a roll in the hay for old times'
sake?" He grabbed her shoulders and attempted to
turn her to face him, his manner stern, his voice demanding. "Answer me, Vicki."

She shook away from his grasp. She did not dare
look at him. If she did, she knew he would be able to
see right through her...right into her very soul.
"Please, Wyatt...please leave right now." Her words
were barely audible.

Anger bristled inside him. "Fifteen years ago
you—"

She whirled around and glared at him, effectively
cutting off anything he might have been about to say.
"Fifteen years ago is history. It's dead and over!"
How dare he bring that up now! Fifteen years ago they
had made love, then he deserted her. He had gotten
what he wanted. That was all she had meant to him.
She turned away, her voice softening as the painful
memory returned. "There's nothing to talk about."

He recognized the stubborn determination on her
face and knew there was no point in continuing the
conversation. He would try later, when things had
calmed down. What he did not know was how and
why things had gotten so out of hand in the last ten
minutes when the previous night had been so won-
derful. It had given him hope for the future, of a life
with Vicki—of having a family of his own rather than
spending his future alone. Now, just as suddenly, his
hopes and plans for the future were once again dashed
and he did not understand why.

He gathered his clothes and dressed. Before leaving,
he paused at the door. "We'll talk about this later,

when you've calmed down.'' He turned and walked out the door into the early morning darkness, then climbed into his car and drove away.

Vicki watched out the living-room window until his taillights had disappeared into the darkness. Finally she turned away and went to the kitchen to make coffee. She tried to force her mind away from what had happened last night by tidying up before Richie came home.

She gathered her clothes from the living-room floor, cleared away the wineglasses and removed the empty condom packets from the nightstand in her bedroom. She hesitated a moment as she stared at the remaining unused packets. Warmth suffused her body as she recalled his words about using as many of them as possible. They had certainly put forth every effort to accomplish just that.

Shaking away the errant thoughts, she picked up the remaining packets and shoved them in the drawer. For a brief moment she had entertained the idea of the three of them being a true family. Wyatt, herself, and Richie—*their* son. But the happy thoughts did not last long. They could never be a real family unless she told her son the truth, and she did not know how she ever would be able to do that. She could not shatter his memories of Robert Bingham as a loving father. Where just a few hours ago she had been filled with warm feelings, she was now filled with sadness for what might have been.

''What's the matter, Mom? You look like you're gonna cry.''

''What?'' She forced a calm demeanor. She had been so absorbed by her own concerns that she had not heard her son come in the door. ''Richie...''

"Is there something wrong?" He carefully scrutinized the living room as he walked in from the kitchen.

"No, nothing's wrong. You startled me, that's all. I didn't hear you come in." She mustered a bit of a smile. "You're home earlier than I thought you'd be. Did you have breakfast at Tim's house? Do you want me to fix you something to eat?"

"Tim's mom fixed us breakfast. I just came home to change clothes. Me and Tim—"

"Tim and I."

"Yeah, okay. *Tim and I* are going to the park to play basketball. I'm supposed to meet him in twenty minutes."

"I'll be leaving for work in a few minutes. I'll see you later."

Vicki checked the time. She needed to hurry to meet the mail truck. She looked forward to a busy day. Maybe that would get her mind off the events of the previous night and what she now realized had been a horrible mistake.

Wyatt's irritation had turned to all-out anger by the time he arrived at his house. He could not understand why Vicki had become so distant and hostile. Last night she had been a warm, giving woman whose love-making was more intense and fulfilling than anything he had ever experienced. But this morning she had turned into an entirely different woman, one he hardly knew. It was as if she could not get him out of her house fast enough.

And there was the fear. He saw it in her eyes again. And again, he did not understand it.

Fifteen years ago they had made love, then she had

disappeared from his life. Last night they had made love and before light the next morning, she had told him to leave. He did not understand any of it.

He took the stairs two at a time and retreated to his bedroom suite, where he took a shower and put on clean clothes. He needed to clear his head and work out his anger, so he headed for the stables. A brisk ride always made him feel better. He saddled a horse and a few minutes later was galloping across the rolling foothills toward the back reaches of his property.

He rode for a couple of hours, forcing his mind to go blank. It was the only way he could blot out thoughts of Vicki and the most incredible night he had spent in many years...possibly the most incredible night ever. It had also been a night that solidified his very deep and very real feelings for her.

For the past fifteen years his life had been empty. He had had external activities and work, but he felt no real purpose or belonging. Then suddenly Vicki was once again part of his reality. Their night together had been very special, and had allowed him to feel whole for the first time since she had left.

He had ridden almost full circle back toward the stables when he reined his horse to a quick stop. His attention had been yanked away from his thoughts by the two dirt bikes leaning against a tree at the entrance to the old caves. He immediately dismounted, and walked toward the cave entrance, leading his horse behind him.

"Hello...is anybody in there?" Wyatt called into the cave without venturing inside. "These caves are unsafe. Come out now." He waited a minute, listening for a response. He was about to call out again when he heard voices coming toward him. A moment later two teenage boys came into sight. He immediately spotted Richie.

"You boys know you're on private property." He looked from one defiant face to the other guilty face. "What about it, Richie? Didn't we have this discussion the other day?"

Richie's guilty look changed to embarrassment as he stared at the ground. "Yeah, I guess we did."

The defiant look on Tim Forsythe's face did not change. "We're not hurting anything."

"It's not a matter of you hurting something. These caves are unstable and therefore dangerous. They need to be blocked off. I didn't realize there was any urgency to the situation, but then I didn't realize anyone was coming out here."

Tim fixed Wyatt with a hard stare. "Who are you to be telling us to get out of here?"

"This is Wyatt Edwards. He owns the place," Richie said quickly, addressing his friend.

Tim whirled around to face Richie, obviously surprised that his friend knew something he did not know. "How do you know this guy?"

"My mom knows him. He was at the store the other day." Wyatt noticed that Richie purposely omitted his earlier run-in with him on the horse trail.

"Yeah, well..." Tim attempted to maintain his tough-guy persona, but it was obvious he was at a loss. "If these caves are so dangerous, why ain't they closed?"

Wyatt stared at Tim, a hard glint in his eye. He wanted to quell Tim's aggressiveness. "If I'd been aware that people were trespassing on private property, I would have done it as soon as I moved back to

Sea Cliff. So, maybe you'd like to take your bike and head back into town now?''

Tim adopted a defiant swagger as he walked toward his bike. "I've seen everything I wanna see. Come on, Rich, let's get out of here and go shoot some hoops.''

"Hold on a minute, Richie. I'd like to talk to you." Wyatt was not sure exactly what he planned to say, but he wanted the opportunity to have some time with Vicki's son without any interruptions.

Richie looked from Wyatt to Tim, then back to Wyatt. He paused for a moment, then turned to Tim. "You go ahead. I'll catch up with you in a little bit."

Tim shot one last look at Wyatt, then got on his bike and rode down the trail.

Richie appraised Wyatt in a critical manner, then spoke. "What do you want?"

Wyatt took a calming breath, then plunged into unknown territory without even a clear-cut plan to help him through. "I thought it might be a nice idea if we got better acquainted.''

"Yeah? Why?" Richie's attitude was not hostile, but cautiously curious.

"Maybe your mother told you. We...we were friends." He was not sure where he was going with the conversation, but he was committed to continue. "It was a long time ago, before she moved away. I've been away myself for several years. I...I didn't know about your grandfather. I was sorry to hear."

"Yeah." A reflective expression covered Richie's features. "I didn't know him very well. He visited us in Dallas a couple of times, but we never came to Sea Cliff...until a couple of months ago when we moved here." He stared at Wyatt for a moment. "How do you know Mom? Did you go to school with her?"

"Not really." An uncomfortable twinge jabbed at his insides in response to the question. "I was four years ahead of her, but this is a small town. Everyone pretty much knew everyone. Besides, your grandfather owned the only market in town and ran the post office, so everyone knew him."

It had been a lousy idea. He could not imagine what had prompted him to ask Richie to stay behind. One thing was very clear. He needed to steer the conversation to another topic, maybe find a common interest of some sort.

He gestured in the direction Tim had gone. "It sounds like you and your friend like basketball. Do you play on the school team?"

"Not this year, but I should be able to make the varsity squad next year. Maybe football, too."

"You like sports? What about horseback riding?" Wyatt took a moment to stroke his horse's neck.

Richie looked at the horse standing quietly at Wyatt's side. "I've been riding a couple of times."

He saw the interest in Richie's eyes in spite of the boy's attempt to suppress any outward show. "Would you like to borrow one of my horses and go riding some time?"

"Really?" Richie's expression brightened at the prospect.

"Sure. How about tomorrow morning?" The uneasiness that had settled in the pit of Wyatt's stomach began to lessen a little. He was relieved to have found some common area of interest between himself and Vicki's son. He had noticed how protective she seemed to be of him. And the way Richie stepped into the argument he and Vicki were having showed that Richie was equally protective of his mother. He knew he would have to win Richie over if he expected to have any sort of a relationship with Vicki. Besides, he liked the boy.

"Yeah, I'd like that." Richie stepped over to the horse and stroked its neck a couple of times. His affinity for the animal was obvious in both his expression and his gesture.

"It's settled then. I'll see you about eight o'clock." Wyatt hesitated for a moment, not sure exactly how to proceed. "How about asking your mom if she'd like to join us? We can take a ride along the beach, then all have lunch together."

Richie cocked his head. His eyes narrowed as he studied Wyatt for a moment. There was something about his expression, about the set of his jaw, that made Wyatt suddenly very uneasy. Then Richie let loose with the bombshell.

"Did you and Mom used to date?"

Six

It was a decidedly pointed question, and it made Wyatt even more uncomfortable than he had been a moment earlier. He recalled Vicki's words about Richie being very perceptive. He tried to sound casual. "What made you ask that?"

Richie shrugged. "Just curious. When I heard the argument you were having the other day, it sounded like the kind of stuff people say when they know each other real good, that's all."

"It was a long time ago when we both lived here. I guess we…uh…might have gone out a couple of times. Maybe to the movies."

Richie stared at Wyatt, then abruptly turned away. An edge of sarcasm clung to his words. "Yeah… right."

Wyatt took a calming breath. He was not sure where Richie's head was, but he did not like the silent signals

emanating from the teenager's sudden change in attitude. He kept his concerns to himself and continued
as if nothing unusual had happened. "Well, I imagine
you want to catch up with your friend. I'll see you in
the morning." He put his boot into the stirrup and
swung up into the saddle. "Don't forget to ask your
mother to come riding with us."

"I don't think she knows anything about riding
horses."

Wyatt grinned at him. "Sure she does."

Richie furrowed his brow, a perplexed expression
on his face. He stared at Wyatt for a minute, then got
on his dirt bike and started down the trail headed toward town.

Wyatt rode back to his stables, his mind occupied
with the time he had just spent with Vicki's son. It
had been an odd encounter. It seemed to him that
Richie was testing him, baiting him, attempting in his
own adolescent way to dig beneath the surface. Did
Richie suspect that there was more of a history between himself and Vicki than either of them were letting on? Did he know about Wyatt being with Vicki
the previous night? Wyatt did not know, but it bothered him. And it was not the only thing he found bothersome.

That sense of something familiar he had from his
first meeting with Richie was now even stronger. He
could not explain it, but he felt a very real connection
between them. Maybe it was just wishful thinking on
his part. After all, Richie was bright, alert, inquisitive,
adventuresome…just the type of son he wished he
could have had. There were so many things he could
do for both Richie and Vicki. Perhaps the possibility
of a future as a family was not so far-fetched after all.

He clenched his jaw into a hard line. The hurt and anger flashed through him again, just as it had when he returned from South America to find that Vicki had moved away and he did not know where she had gone…or why. Were his jumbled emotions nothing more than the bittersweet recognition that had things been different Richie could have been—*should* have been—their son?

The tension began to drain from his body as his thoughts turned to the night before, to the burning passion that had passed between Vicki and him. He allowed a frown to wrinkle his forehead as he also recalled the way she had suddenly changed that morning—becoming nervous, anxious…and distant. It was more than concern that Richie might find him at her house so early in the morning. It was the same fear he had seen in her ever since his return.

He handed his horse over to Fred Olson and returned to the house. After he had cleaned up and changed clothes, he went to the office wing to take care of some paperwork. It was close to three o'clock when he pushed back from his desk.

A restlessness churned inside him. He wandered aimlessly through the house. He paused in the front entryway and stared up the two stories to the cathedral ceiling with the crystal chandelier. Even with an entire wing converted to office space, the house was still too large for one person. There should be a family living in the house. His gaze traveled slowly across the living room. And Vicki should be part of that family.

An inner drive, a need to make his life whole again, seemed to be controlling his actions—the same inner need that had dictated his return to Sea Cliff. Without giving it any conscious thought, he found himself sitting in his car outside Vicki's place of business. He entered through the post-office door, checked his mail, then walked into the market. Vicki and Noreen were both busy, so he hung around the magazine rack, killing time by looking at various periodicals. It was almost twenty minutes before things slowed down.

Vicki looked up and spotted Wyatt. She had not seen him come in. She nervously looked around to see who else was in the store. She could not stop her errant thoughts and feelings, the ones that relived each and every moment of passion they had shared the previous night, the ones that told her she could not deny her love for Wyatt Edwards...and how forbidden that love was. She had allowed—*encouraged* would be more accurate—their lovemaking, knowing full well that it could not happen again no matter how much she wanted it to be so.

The ringing phone grabbed her attention, but Noreen picked it up before Vicki could reach it. As soon as Noreen commenced what was obviously a personal conversation, Wyatt made his way toward Vicki. He poured himself a cup of coffee, then reached into his pocket for money, placing it next to the cash register.

He took a sip from his cup. "Have you had a busy day? You look a little frazzled."

His blue eyes sparkled. His dazzling smile totally unnerved her in the way it reached out to her desires. She immediately felt her iron resolve melt away, leaving her totally vulnerable to his considerable sex appeal and charm.

"I look frazzled?" Her gaze darted nervously around the store. She ran her fingers through her hair, attempting to collect her composure. "I probably could use a touch of lipstick and a few moments to run a comb through my hair.''

He placed his fingertips beneath her chin to draw her attention to him. "I was referring to your behavior rather than your appearance," he said, his words soft, smooth and very sensuous. He trailed his fingers down the side of her neck. "You look beautiful. In fact," he went on, warming to the idea that circulated through his mind, "you look like you need to be whisked away to some secluded beach—"

"Just what is that supposed to mean?" She snapped out of her sensual daze and glared at him. Was he mocking her by referring to the beach at the cove where they had made love for the first time? Had the previous night been just a game for Wyatt? Had he seduced her for no more reason than to see if he could?

Then she saw the shocked expression on his face and did not know what to think. She blinked a couple of times and took a step back as she tried to clear her thoughts.

Wyatt's expression changed from surprise to exasperation as he folded his arms across his chest. He leveled a hard look at her. "What the hell's going on here, Vicki? You're a bundle of nerves—one minute you're as frightened as a trapped animal and the next, as aggressive as a mother lion defending her cub. I thought that last night we had—"

"Last night was a mistake. I told you that this morning." Her words were flat, said without conviction or enthusiasm.

He started to grab her by the shoulders, then backed off when he remembered that they were not alone. Noreen was still busy with her phone conversation, but two customers had come in the front door. He lowered his voice to just above a whisper, but the edge was still there. "Last night was no mistake, Vicki." He lowered his head and stared at the floor for a moment, gathering his thoughts. His manner softened as the warm memory of their lovemaking filled his senses. He raised his head and fixed her with a level gaze. "We were good together fifteen years ago, and we were good together last night."

Vicki's anger resurfaced. "I told you, we have nothing to talk about that concerns fifteen years ago. That was then and it's over." Why did he have to keep bringing up the past? Hadn't he hurt her enough fifteen years ago? Did he have to do it again?

Then another thought occurred to her. Could it be he suspected the truth about Richie?

"There was nothing about last night that in any way indicates to me that things are over."

The front door of the market opened and Richie walked in bouncing a basketball. He stopped when he saw Wyatt and Vicki obviously engaged in another argument. He stood just inside the door, staring at them, as he continued to bounce the ball.

Vicki turned toward her son. "How many times have I told you not to bounce that ball in here? I don't want to have to tell you again." Her words came out with more irritation that she had intended.

Richie looked at her curiously. "Sure, Mom. You don't need to get all bent out of shape." He tucked the ball under his arm, shot a quick glance at Wyatt, then returned his attention to Vicki. "Did Wyatt talk to you about the horseback riding?"

Wyatt saw the startled expression cover her face, then change to confusion. She could hardly get out the words. ''Horseback riding? What...what are you talking about?''

''This morning, when we were talking, Wyatt asked me if I wanted to go horseback riding tomorrow. He said to ask you to go with us.''

Vicki reached out and grabbed hold of the counter to steady herself. She could not have heard Richie correctly. She shook her head in an effort to clear the cobwebs, and tried her best to speak calmly. ''You...uh...you and...uh...Wyatt were together this morning?'' She tried again to force the quaver out of her voice. ''How did this happen? I thought you were at the park playing basketball with Tim.''

An almost overwhelming foreboding swept through her. Wyatt and her son had spent time together...alone. That was something she had been determined to prevent. No good could come from the two of them becoming friends, from Wyatt learning too much about Richie. It was the one thing that truly frightened her above all else. But was she already too late?

Wyatt was both fascinated and confused by the very real terror that played across Vicki's face and surrounded her words. A moment earlier she had been angry for no apparent reason and now she seemed to be fighting to maintain some semblance of control over her fear. But fear of what?

Wyatt gave her an encouraging smile. ''Yes, Richie and I are going riding in the morning and I'd like you to join us. Is eight o'clock okay with you? We can have lunch afterward.''

''I...'' Vicki blanched and visibly trembled. No, it simply could not be. She did not want to believe that her secret was starting to come to light so soon. Somewhere in the back of her mind she knew there was a very real possibility that everything would come out anyway, but not now...not yet.

"What's the matter, Mom? You look white as a ghost." Richie's worried expression echoed his words.

"Are you okay, Vicki?" Wyatt reached across the counter and cupped her elbow in an offer of support. His concern matched Richie's.

"I'm fine." She pulled away from Wyatt's touch as quickly as possible without being too obvious. His presence was disconcerting enough without physical contact between them.

Wyatt brushed away her attempt to dislodge his hand from her elbow. "You don't *look* fine. Do you want to sit down?" He turned toward Richie. "Get your mother a glass of water while I help her back to the office."

"Sure thing." Richie grabbed one of the cups next to the coffeepot and filled it from the water cooler.

As soon as Vicki and Wyatt were away from Richie, she jerked her arm out of his grasp. "I'm fine. I don't need any help and I don't need to sit down. I was...uh, just a little surprised that Richie had been with you this morning. He told me he was going to the park to play basketball."

"Don't you think you're being overly protective? He's not a little boy anymore."

As soon as the words were out of his mouth, he knew he should not have said them.

She spoke through clenched teeth. "I don't need any advice from you about anything, least of all about how to raise my son. I realize this is a small town and it probably isn't as necessary for me to keep as close

an eye on him as I did in Dallas, but I'm still his
mother and he should let me know where he's going."

"Give it a rest, Mom. Stop treating me like a kid!"
Richie's words were defiant. His body language and
tone of voice said this was not a new topic of discussion between them. "It was no big deal."

Richie calmed down from his outburst and handed
her the glass of water. "We started to play basketball,
then ended up exploring an old cave in the hills. That's
where we ran into Wyatt."

She tried to maintain an outer calm while placing
herself between her son who seemed to be growing up
too quickly and the man she needed to keep at a distance. She knew she was walking a tightrope without
benefit of a safety net, but she did not know what else
to do. She was in too deep to turn around now.

"I see." She reached out to smooth back Richie's
hair, but withdrew her hand as soon as she saw the
look on his face. "Well…" She nervously cleared her
throat. "I hope you boys didn't bother Wyatt by
traipsing around his property uninvited."

Wyatt quickly stepped into the conversation.
"There wasn't any harm done. My only concern was
that the cave is unstable. It needs to be closed off,
something I just instructed Fred to handle. I explained
the situation to Richie and his friend and that was the
end of it."

Wyatt shifted his weight to the other foot and also
shifted the focus of the conversation. "Now, let's get
back to something more important. Richie mentioned
it before I had a chance to, but let me follow up. We're
going horseback riding in the morning and it would
be nice if you could join us." He cocked his head and

offered her an encouraging smile. "How about it? See you at eight o'clock?"

She felt trapped. She looked at her son, and could tell by his expression that he was looking forward to it. Spending time with Wyatt certainly was not the most prudent thing for her to do. However, allowing her son to spend time with him alone was even less prudent. Something as simple as Wyatt asking Richie when his birthday was and how old he would be could spell disaster. "Eight o'clock is fine."

Wyatt noted her lack of enthusiasm. It was almost as if she was being forced into doing something she did not want to do. It was odd. If she truly did not want to go, then why had she agreed? She seemed to be on an emotional roller coaster. Each time he came in contact with her it became more puzzling. In fact, he had not understood anything about her behavior from the day he returned home so many years ago and found out she had moved away without even a good-bye.

"Well, I guess I'd better be going. I'll see you in the morning, Richie." He grasped Vicki's hand and gave it a little squeeze, then let it go. His voice softened. "I'll see you in the morning, too."

After putting away the dinner dishes, Vicki settled into her favorite chair with a book. Richie stood in the kitchen door staring at her—to the point where she became very uneasy. She finally looked up at him. "What's the matter, Richie? Is there something wrong?"

He crossed the room. "That's what I want to know. You've been acting real weird the last few days...ever since Wyatt showed up." He eyed her suspiciously.

SHAWNA DELACORTE 107

"What's with you and him? I asked him if the two of you used to date, but he just blew me off with some dumb answer." He fixed her with a direct stare. "So what gives?"

Her heart thudded in her chest and she experienced a sudden shortness of breath. She knew she was on the edge of an anxiety attack, but she had to get herself under control. She could not let Richie see her distress. Trying to collect her wits, she said, "You…uh, why would you have asked him that?"

"I was curious, that's all. So what's the big deal? Why should everyone get all bent out of shape over one little question?"

Vicki's thoughts were frantic and scattered. Did Richie suspect something? That was a dumb question. Of course he suspected something or he would not have asked the question to begin with.

"What did Wyatt tell you?" She could not control the nervousness in her voice.

His eyes narrowed as he leveled a suspicious gaze at her. "Why do you want to know? Is your answer going to be different from his?"

She saw the defiance on his face and heard the skepticism in his voice. "I don't think I like your tone or your attitude, young man."

"Well…" He relented, but only for a moment. Then he quickly regained his determination. "I don't think I like getting the runaround, either. Something's going on between you two. Why is everybody getting so nervous just because I asked if you and Wyatt ever dated? I mean, that was a long time ago. Clear back before you even met Dad, right?"

"Well, that's true. I didn't meet Robert until I moved to Dallas."

"So, you and Wyatt dated before you knew Dad and you're dating again now. What's the big deal and why all the secrets?"

Vicki looked at Richie, but she saw Wyatt—Wyatt's eyes, his handsome features, his coloring…and the same type of stubborn determination. Her son was, indeed, becoming an adult who could no longer be put off with simple answers meant only to appease and distract a child.

She emitted a heavy sigh of resignation and set her book on the coffee table. Just how much should she tell him? She turned it over in her mind, then made her decision. "Sit down, Richie. You're right. You are old enough and I should be treating you more like an adult."

A nervousness appeared in Richie's eyes, an uncertainty that said he was no longer sure he wanted to know what was going on. He sat down on the couch.

"I've never told you anything about our family history. It all started with my grandfather—your great-grandfather—and Wyatt's grandfather." She filled him in on the land deal, what had happened, the family feud that had ensued, and how it had related to Wyatt and her. "We had gone out a couple of times, but there was a considerable amount of pressure on us from both families. And…well, it just didn't work out."

Richie sat quietly, apparently digesting what he had just heard. After a few minutes he looked up at his mother. "Do you mean that the land back in the hills, maybe even where the cave is, should really be yours now?"

She thought for a moment. "I don't know how to answer that question. I don't really know exactly what belonged to my grandfather before he and Wyatt's grandfather entered into their business deal.''

"So...is that why you and Wyatt argue all the time?"

"What makes you say that?" She laughed nervously. Once again, she did not know how to answer his very perceptive question. "Wyatt and I don't spend our time arguing." She bit at her lower lip as she tried to put her thoughts in order. "Oh, we may have had a couple of exchanges of words, but nothing I would call an argument."

Richie stood up, the anger and defiance returning to his face and showing in his tone of voice. "I thought we agreed that you were going to treat me like an adult instead of a kid. That agreement didn't last very long, did it?"

"I don't know what you're talking about—"

"Yeah...right." Richie grabbed his jacket. "I'm going to Tim's." He turned and slammed out the front door.

Vicki jumped to her feet and hurried to the door. She yanked it open and started to yell at him to come back, but caught herself before she said anything. She watched as he walked down the street toward the Forsythe house. He was right. She had not been totally honest with him. But she could not tell him the complete truth any more than she could confide it to Wyatt. The secret was hers alone and she would have to find a way to live with it.

She returned to her book, but was unable to concentrate on it. After reading the same page four times, she set the book aside. She watched the news on television then went to bed, but could not fall asleep. She remained awake until she heard Richie come home.

Her first instinct was to get up and talk to him about what had happened. Then she thought better of it. What would she say to him? She could either tell him the truth or dig a deeper hole with yet another lie. Neither option was acceptable, so she stayed in bed and did battle with the anxiety churning in her stomach. Finally, long after midnight, she managed to sleep.

The next morning Richie had showered, dressed and was in the kitchen looking for something to eat before Vicki got out of bed. She finally made her way into the kitchen and started the coffee.

She was surprised by her son's flurry of activity. "You're certainly up early."

"We're going horseback riding this morning, remember?"

"Oh, yes..." She nervously cleared her throat. "I don't think—"

He stopped what he was doing and leveled a serious look in her direction. "You don't have to go if you don't want to, but I'm going."

It was a definitive statement. Vicki could see that, short of absolutely forbidding him to go, there was nothing she could do to dissuade him, and she had no valid reason for saying no. She could not allow Richie to spend the time alone with Wyatt, especially not now that he was asking questions. She could not take a chance on him continuing to question Wyatt as he had questioned her. She also could not take a chance on Richie repeating the story she had told him.

She would go with them. There was no other way. "I'll hurry and get ready."

Before long they were on their way to Wyatt's

house. She pulled her car into the circular drive, and sat for a moment staring at the impressive edifice. It was the first time in fifteen years that she had been on the hill. A little tremor of apprehension started in her stomach and worked its way outward.

"Are we going to sit in the car all day?" Richie's impatience cut through her preoccupation.

"No, of course not." She opened the car door and slid out from behind the wheel.

The front door of the house swung open and Wyatt stepped out on the porch. "Good morning," he called out. He bounded down the front steps, the picture of enthusiasm and energy. He reached Vicki's car just as Richie opened the door and got out, heading for the house. "It's good to see you again, Richie."

When he turned his attention to Vicki, his voice softened with an intimacy that spoke almost as loudly as his words. "I'm glad you decided to join us."

"Well...I, uh, it seemed like—" She bit at her lower lip as she ran her fingers through her hair. She needed to get herself under control, put a lid on her soaring fears and concerns. She turned to look out across the valley to the ocean. The panorama of mountains, cliffs and ocean always brought with it a sense of calm. "I've always loved this view."

Wyatt studied her as she scanned the horizon. Something about her manner held a silent warning that left him feeling decidedly uncomfortable. He tried to project an upbeat demeanor. "I think we have the perfect morning for a ride. It's a nice, sunny day with a hint of autumn's crispness. What do you think?"

"Yes," she said without enthusiasm, "it's a nice day."

His tone softened, and his words were for her ears

only. "I'm really glad you decided to come along. It will be just like old times, riding along the beach—''

She answered just as quietly. "I'm only here because...well, because Richie asked me to join the two of you." She turned to face Wyatt. "That's the only reason." She quickly looked away. She could not deal with the myriad of emotions she saw displayed in his eyes.

Wyatt felt as if he had been slapped in the face. His words were sharp, bordering on angry. "I don't know what's going on with you, Vicki. You seem to be going up and down like a yo-yo. One minute we're making love with a passion and intensity that far surpasses anything I've ever experienced and the next minute you turn away from me as if I am your worst nightmare. No one forced you to be here. If my company is so distasteful to you, then you're free to leave. I can drive Richie home after lunch.'' He had been patient. He had exhibited extreme tolerance for her weird behavior, but the bottom line was that he was the injured party and she was treating him as if he had done something wrong.

"That's not what I meant—"

"I heard every word you said and it doesn't take a genius to figure out what you meant.'' Wyatt straightened up and stuck his hands in his pockets. His expression totally hid whatever was going on inside him.

She fought to hold back the tears caused by his unexpected reaction. He had nearly destroyed her life when he walked out on her and now he was treating her as if she was the one who had done something wrong. "You're jumping to—"

"Hey!" Richie shouted at them from the porch, his words cutting off the heated exchange that had not been loud enough to reach his ears. "Are we going to ride horses, or are you two going to stand there and whisper all morning?"

Wyatt turned to him and forced a smile, "Let's head for the stables. Fred should have the horses saddled and waiting." He glanced back toward Vicki, his smile fading as he noted her tightly clenched jaw and harsh expression.

His words held an edge that matched her attitude. "Are you coming with us, Vicki, or do you prefer to stay here?"

"Uh...yes, of course I'm going with you." She turned and walked with Wyatt and Richie to the stables.

The horse trail led across the foothills and down to a stretch of beach along the mouth of a creek. Wyatt and Vicki had ridden it several times in years gone by, and now there were three of them. The circumstances and situation were old, yet they were also new. If Vicki had not been so frightened of what the future might hold, it would have been a perfect day.

She became more and more fearful as she watched Wyatt and Richie together. They seemed to have a natural affinity and that was going to make it even more difficult for her to keep them apart. Richie's riding expertise was limited, and Wyatt gave him several tips on how to handle the horse. Richie was obviously having a good time and Wyatt seemed to be enjoying himself, but Vicki was miserable. She knew her son needed a male role model in his life, someone who could help guide a teenage boy through the turbulent years ahead. From the look of things, it seemed that Richie had made the selection himself. He had chosen Wyatt.

Again Vicki questioned what was worse, denying Wyatt the knowledge that he had a son or destroying her son's security in his memories of the only father he had ever known.

And then there were her own needs. She loved Wyatt. She always had and she knew she always would. But her son came first. If only she could figure out the right thing to do.

After the ride they returned to the stables to deposit the horses. Lunch had been prepared at the house and set out on the back patio.

"This looks great. I'm starved." Richie seated himself at the table without waiting for anyone else. He was joined a moment later by Vicki and Wyatt.

Vicki picked at her food, shoving most of it around her plate with her fork. She watched Richie—the way he laughed, the enthusiasm he exhibited. The bond forming between her son and Wyatt would have been obvious to even the most casual of observers. And it was tearing her apart inside.

Wyatt pushed back from the table after finishing lunch. "Richie…how would you like to go down to the stables and have Fred teach you how to groom a horse?"

Richie's face brightened and his eyes sparkled. "Yeah?"

"Sure. Why don't you go on and we'll be down in a little bit?"

Richie jumped up from his chair and hurried off toward the stables. As soon as he was out of sight, Wyatt turned his attention to Vicki. His expression was stern.

"Okay, Vicki. What's going on here? You haven't

said half a dozen words in the last four hours. You only picked at your lunch.'' He placed his fingertips beneath her chin, lifted it slightly, then studied her for a moment. Abruptly his attitude softened and he brushed his fingers across the smoothness of her cheek, then cupped her chin in the palm of his hand. ''Talk to me, Vicki. Tell me what's wrong. You look like your greatest fear is about to gobble you up and swallow you whole.''

Seven

Vicki knew that Wyatt had no way of knowing exactly how true his words were, how closely they hit home. She could barely respond. "Don't, Wyatt." She pulled back. "Please don't." She did not pull back far enough to dislodge his hand.

"Don't what?" He drew her up from her chair and folded her into his embrace. A moment later his mouth was on hers.

She put up a struggle, but only for a second or two. Then she melted into the passion of his kiss. She could no more resist his sexual magnetism than the moth could resist the flame. Her body trembled as she put her arms around his neck and openly welcomed his warmth and sensuality.

He ran his fingers through her hair before cradling the back of her head in the palm of his hand. He ran his other hand across her shoulder, then down her back, and pressed the length of his body against hers.

She was everything he wanted.

She was all he wanted.

A moment later their tongues entwined and his mouth filled with her taste. He wanted more of her, much more. He ran his hand across the curve of her hip, then cupped her bottom, settling her hips against his. A searing heat passed between them, the same type of heat as the other night when they had made love.

Vicki came to her senses in time to put a stop to his brazen daylight seduction. "Wyatt…" She slipped out of his arms and took a couple of steps away from his all-too-tempting nearness. She tried to cover her flustered condition, to catch her breath, but to no avail. "This is…a mistake. I need to find Richie…we have to go home…he has schoolwork to do.…"

Before she could say anything else he swept her back into his arms. "This is no mistake. It wasn't a mistake fifteen years ago and it's certainly not a mistake now."

She stiffened and tore herself away from his embrace. With the single exception of the gift of her son, fifteen years ago had been a horrible mistake. She could not let her feelings for Wyatt cloud the truth of what had happened, of the way he had walked out on her. A person who hadn't learned from past mistakes was a person doomed to repeat those mistakes. Well, she had learned from hers.

"I told you I don't want to dredge up the past. It's over. How many times do I need to tell you before you get it through your head?" She avoided looking at him, knowing full well that it would not take very much effort on his part to have her back in his arms again. The only way to keep that from happening was to get away from him. She reached for her jacket on the back of the chair. "I'd better find Richie so we can leave. I need to check the store to make sure things are okay."

Hurrying off the patio and across the lawn before he could stop her, she went straight to the stables. She had located Richie and was turning to leave just as Wyatt entered.

Wyatt swallowed his anger rather than create a scene in front of Richie. He took a calming breath. "I have an idea, Vicki. I understand about you needing to take care of your business, but that doesn't mean Richie has to leave. Why don't you let him stay? I can bring him home later."

Richie jumped at the opening. "Yeah, Mom. I can stay here and help Fred with the horses."

She bit at her lower lip as she tried to gain composure. "I think it's best that we leave, Richie. Fred has work to do and Wyatt is a busy man. I'm sure he has several things that require his attention. And you have schoolwork to do—"

"No, I don't. I already did my homework. Why can't I stay? Wyatt said he'd take me home, so you won't have to come get me."

"Well...I just think it would be better if you..." Her voice trailed off. She did not have any valid reason for saying no. None, that is, except her own fears of what would be said when Richie and Wyatt were alone together. She did not know what to do.

Richie looked at her curiously. "It would be better if I what?"

"I…uh…just don't want you monopolizing Wyatt's time, that's all. He has a company to run and—"

"It's Sunday, Vicki. I've given myself the day off. I don't have a company to run until tomorrow. So, unless you have some other reason, I don't see why Richie can't learn about taking care of the horses. That way, whenever he wants to go riding he'll know what has to be done."

"I…" She glanced nervously around the inside of the stables. Fred Olson leaned against the stall railing, listening to every word being said. "Well, I guess you've wiped out all of my objections."

A warm smile spread across Wyatt's face. "I knew we could come to some reasonable understanding."

"Come on, Richie," Fred urged. "I'll show ya the tack room."

Vicki watched as Fred and Richie left the stables. An uneasiness settled in her stomach. She had not known what else to say. She could see how excited Richie was, how much he wanted to stay. To have denied her son permission now would have meant saying something meaningless like *you can't stay because I say so* and that was not the type of relationship she had with Richie.

She had always made it a point to explain to him exactly why she made certain decisions so he would understand that it was not just an arbitrary choice. But there was no way she could explain to him her reasons for insisting that he leave—not this time. He was growing up, but she was sure he was not mature enough to understand any of this.

Wyatt interrupted her thoughts with a brand-new concern for her to contend with. "It seems that we have the afternoon to ourselves…unless you really do need to leave.''

"I should be leaving…" Regardless of her earlier statements, she knew she did not dare leave Richie and Wyatt alone. Had he anticipated that? Was he counting on it? "But I suppose I could stay until Richie is ready to go. I wouldn't want to inconvenience you in driving him home."

Deeper and deeper. It was beginning to look as if she would never be able to stop the downward spiral of lies.

Vicki spent a very uncomfortable afternoon. She stayed as far away from Wyatt's all-too-tempting touch as possible without being obvious about it. She did not dare allow even a hint of impropriety in front of her son.

It was late afternoon when she and Richie left the stables. Richie's excitement and enthusiasm filled the car as they drove home. "That was great. Wyatt said I could go horseback riding anytime I wanted to and Fred showed me all about saddling a horse and about grooming them."

"You…uh…really like Wyatt, don't you?"

"Yeah." Richie turned to face her as she drove. "I don't know why you guys always get into arguments. I think he's great."

"Yes, he certainly can be quite charming when he wants to." She could not stop the shiver that ran through her body. It was too late. There was nothing she could do to keep Richie and Wyatt apart. Everything seemed to be closing in around her. How long would it be before someone made a comment about the physical resemblance between them? How long before she had to come up with some hard answers? How long would it be before Wyatt figured out that Richie was his son?

The next couple of days were quiet for Vicki, as she returned to the routine that existed before Wyatt Edwards burst on the scene and threw her life into turmoil. In fact, she did not see Wyatt at all. Even in the short time since his return to Sea Cliff, she had become accustomed to having him show up on a daily basis. But maybe she had been able to discourage him to the point where he would not be hanging around anymore.

As if on cue, Wyatt strolled in the front door of the market looking incredibly handsome and head-to-toe desirable. "Good afternoon, Vicki." He radiated pure sex appeal and charm as he leaned against the counter.

Vicki closed her eyes for a second in an attempt to gather her wits about her. How easy it was for him. All he had to do was flash that dazzling smile and her insides immediately turned into malleable putty. She purposely forced a noncommittal flatness to her expression and tone. "Good afternoon."

"Well, that greeting certainly lacked enthusiasm." His blue eyes twinkled with wry humor and a sly grin tugged at the corners of his mouth. "If I didn't know better, I'd think you weren't too happy to see me." He glanced around the store to verify that they were alone, then leaned over the counter and placed a quick kiss on her mouth...quick, but decidedly heated. A kiss that said there was a whole lot more.

"I stopped by to invite you to dinner tonight. As soon as you close the market we can drive into the city." He brushed his fingertips across her cheek, then tucked a loose tendril of hair behind her ear. As his eyes searched her face, his expression turned serious and his voice soft. "How about it?"

She took a step back from him. "Either you're kidding or you're being far too presumptuous."

"Oh?" He cocked his head and raised an eyebrow. "What makes you say so?"

She busied herself straightening some papers, then grabbed a towel to wipe the counter. "I have things to do. I'm not just sitting around waiting for you to show up."

He took the towel away from her and placed his hand on top of hers to still her sudden flurry of activity. "What things?"

"Well…" She nervously bit at her lower lip. "It's late afternoon. Richie will be home from school any minute. I have to fix his dinner and then—"

"Okay." He ran his fingers across the back of her hand, up her arm, then cupped her chin. "How about the three of us going to dinner together?"

"What?" Her eyes widened in genuine surprise. "This is a school night. Richie has homework to do. There isn't time to drive twenty miles into the city, have a leisurely dinner, and drive the twenty miles back here."

"All right. Let's talk about this weekend. How about Saturday night for dinner?"

She took a calming breath. "This isn't any good, Wyatt. We can't start again. I've changed. I'm not the same person you knew." She swallowed hard to drive down the hurt that tried to force its way to the surface. What a gullible child she had been to have thought that he had loved her—that was a mistake she would not repeat. "I have numerous responsibilities that leave me no time for—"

"Hi, Mom. When's dinner going to—" Richie stopped in midsentence, and his expression brightened. "Hi, Wyatt."

"Hello, Richie. How's it going?"

"Great!" Richie grabbed a soft drink from the case. "How about you?" He popped the top on the can, took a long swig, then turned his attention to his mother without waiting for Wyatt to answer. He bubbled over with enthusiasm. "Tim's dad is taking him camping this weekend and they invited me to go. We're going to leave first thing Saturday morning and we'll be home Sunday night. All I need to take is my sleeping bag and clothes. Tim's dad has the tent and all that other stuff."

"Well, I don't know, Richie. This is pretty sudden." She glanced nervously toward Wyatt, then back to her son. She saw the disappointment forming on Richie's face.

Robert and Richie had done so many things together. Every month they would do what Robert referred to as *father-and-son projects...no women allowed.* She knew how much Richie missed those outings, the closeness the two of them had shared. It was one of the areas where she had not been able to fill in for Robert.

She smiled lovingly at her son. "Sure. You go and have a good time." She reached out and smoothed his hair away from his face.

He brushed her hand away. "Cut it out, Mom." Richie grabbed a small bag of potato chips and ripped it open.

"Why don't you go on home and start your school-work? I'll be along in a little bit."

"Okay." Shoving a handful of chips in his mouth, Richie headed for the door.

Wyatt had been following the conversation with keen interest. He watched as Richie left the market and walked down the sidewalk toward home. Then he turned his attention back to Vicki. "It seems that you're now free on Saturday, so I'll expect you at my house for dinner as soon as you close the market."

"I don't think so, Wyatt. This isn't a good idea at all. I don't—"

He took her hand in his and led her out from behind the counter and toward her office at the back of the store. She wiggled her hand free of his grasp. "I'm here alone. I need to stay up front."

"Nonsense." He recaptured her hand. "You can hear the buzzer when someone comes in the door." He pulled her into the office and into his arms.

"I've been buried in a new project for the company and this is the first chance I've had to get away from the computer and fax machine," he said softly, his voice carrying an almost hypnotic quality. He traced her upper lip with the tip of his finger. "Do you have any idea how difficult it was for me to keep my mind on work?"

"Wyatt…stop, please don't…" Her determination not to succumb to his charm and magnetism a second time melted away the moment his lips touched the side of her neck.

"Please don't what?" He kissed the tender spot behind her ear, then his mouth found hers.

Her arms went around his neck, as his hands ca-ressed her shoulders. All the heat that had existed before burst into flame once again as her resolve disappeared in a puff of smoke. He was too tempting, too close and she wanted him too much.

Their moment of passion lasted only a few seconds before the sound of the front-door buzzer interrupted them. Someone had entered the store.

She quickly pulled back from him. Her slightly flustered manner told of her embarrassment. ''There's someone in the market. I...I, uh, need to tend to business.'' She left the office without waiting for him to answer.

Alice Thackery's pinched face greeted Vicki as she hurried toward the front counter.

''Victoria,'' Alice said, glancing around the store, ''I was beginning to think you had left your business unattended.''

''I...'' Vicki gestured absently over her shoulder. ''I was in the office. What may I do for you?''

''I have a few items here on my list.'' Alice began taking her selections from the shelves and putting them into her basket.

''Vicki...'' Wyatt's voice came from the rear of the store. ''I've got to get back to work. I'll see you Saturday evening...'' His words trailed off as soon as he spotted Alice Thackery. He nodded curtly. ''Good afternoon, Alice.''

Returning his attention to Vicki, he smiled warmly. ''We can continue our conversation a little later.'' Then he left through the post-office exit to avoid the necessity of passing Alice on his way to the front door.

Vicki turned toward Alice Thackery. A little tremor of apprehension passed through her body when she saw the way the older woman was staring after Wyatt, her eyes narrowed and her mouth pursed. It was the same way she had stared at him before. Was it possible that Alice had been studying his features and comparing them to Richie's, or were her fears just fueling her imagination? Either way she did not like it.

Alice brought her purchases to the counter. She said pointedly, "I understand you and your son spent the day at the Edwards' house last Sunday."

Vicki clenched her jaw for a moment to stop the angry words that immediately leapt to mind. She forced herself to be calm before speaking. "Yes, we did, Mrs. Thackery."

The older woman eyed her skeptically. "Do you think that was wise, considering Wyatt Edwards is probably—"

"Is probably *what,* Mrs. Thackery?" Vickie drew herself up to her full height and glared at the unpleasant little woman. "If you have something specific to say, then say it. Otherwise please confine your conversation to business matters."

"I resent your attitude, Victoria. You have no right to speak to me in that fashion." Alice paid for her purchases and huffed out of the market.

With a sinking feeling, Vicki watched as the older woman walked down the sidewalk toward her house. Just as sure as she knew her own name, she knew Alice Thackery was going to cause her trouble. Small-town gossip could be very cruel. She was confident that she could withstand whatever scandal might arise, but she was not so sure about Richie. The last thing she wanted was for her son to have to contend with any more complications to his life.

Vicki stood on her front porch and waved goodbye to Richie as he left for his camping weekend. She peered through the gray light of dawn as the Forsythe car drove down the street and around the corner. Besides Richie and Tim Forsythe, there were three other boys along for the trip. Richie had been so excited, he'd woken up an hour before it was time to leave, rather than Vicki having to force him to get up that early.

She allowed her mind to turn to the things that Wyatt and Richie could do, the father-and-son projects they could share. Wyatt seemed to genuinely enjoy Richie's company and she had seen the way her son had latched on to Wyatt. Her eyes misted as the tears began to well. She blinked them away and went back inside the house. They were useless thoughts of things that could never be. Wyatt had hurt her before. She had believed in him and he had left her. She would not allow her son to be caught in that same web.

She leaned back against the closed door. Suddenly the tears came again, this time trickling down her cheeks. She tried to swallow away the sobs, but to no avail. She indulged the overwhelming feeling of sorrow for a few minutes, then pulled herself together. She needed to get ready for work.

She had reluctantly agreed to have dinner with Wyatt at his house that night. She wished she was able to be stronger, but she could not resist his very persuasive manner or disregard her own very insistent desires. She knew she was playing with fire. Would she end up regretting her decision? She was sure she would.

Saturday seemed to be suffering from the same indecision as Vicki. One minute the day crawled along, then the next minute time passed far too quickly. One minute she anxiously anticipated dinner with Wyatt

and the next wondered if it was too late to cancel.
Finally, at the end of the business day, she closed and
locked the market door.

She walked home, took a quick shower and dressed
for dinner—three times. She discarded her first choice
of jeans and a sweater as being too casual, but her
second choice of a dress and high heels seemed too
formal. She finally settled on a pair of tailored slacks
and a silk blouse, and did a final check of her appearance in the full-length mirror. Then there was
nothing left to do but drive to Wyatt's house.

She attempted to still the thousands of butterflies
doing battle in her stomach, but it was a useless effort.
With a sigh, she pulled out of the garage and drove
down the street.

Wyatt was a mass of nervous energy as he paced
up and down the front hall. He checked his watch. It
had only been three minutes since he had called
Vicki's house. There had been no answer, which could
only mean that she was on her way. He could not stand
the waiting any longer. He opened the front door and
stood out on the porch staring down the long driveway.

It was a strange sort of nervousness. It was not as
though this was the first time they had seen each other
in fifteen years, neither of them knowing what to expect. Just a week earlier they had spent an incredible
night making love with all the intensity and passion
possible between two people. Yet this felt somehow
different.

There was an uncertainty in the air and it was not
just his uncertainty. Vicki had been acting so strangely
ever since the night they'd made love. Her behavior

had been all over the place—one minute warm and comfortable, and the next minute hostile and distant. He had tried his best to be understanding and supportive while at the same time attempting to deal with his own inner turmoil. But he had finally reached the end of his rope. He fully intended to see to it that she remained at his house until she had provided him with some answers.

His thoughts were interrupted by the sight of headlights moving up the driveway toward the house. He felt the tension drain from his body as he watched her car approach. His heart beat a little faster and his breath came a little easier. He walked down the front steps as she pulled up in front of the porch.

Wyatt opened the driver's door and took her hand to help her out. He kept hold of her hand and pulled her to him. His warm breath tickled across her cheek and his soft words floated across her ear. "I was beginning to worry. I was afraid you had changed your mind."

Vicki wished she felt half as relaxed as Wyatt looked. At one point while driving up the hill she had almost turned back. "I must admit that I thought about it."

"I'm glad you're here." He brushed a tender kiss against her lips, then escorted her inside the house.

A sharp jab of trepidation settled on top of the almost unbearable anxiety inside her. Why should she feel any different tonight than a week ago? There was still just as much at stake, except that during the intervening week Richie and Wyatt had formed a bond. It was not yet a tight bond, perhaps not even a lasting bond, but a week ago it was not there and now it was.

As soon as she stepped into the front entry hall, she

came to an abrupt halt. Last Sunday the three of them had eaten outside on the patio. This was the first time in fifteen years that she had been inside the house. Right here in the foyer was where her world had fallen apart. Right here, Henry Edwards had informed her that Wyatt had left Sea Cliff in an effort to get away from her.

Panic took control of her. She whirled around toward the front door. "I can't do this." The fears, the pain, the years of not understanding what had happened or why—it all came crashing together inside her with such force that she could not contain it. Tears filled her eyes and a sob caught in her throat. "I don't know what kind of a game you're playing or why you're doing this to me, but I refuse to be a part of it any longer."

Wyatt could not have been more shocked if she had physically struck him. He saw the very real anguish clouding her features. He saw the tears spill from her eyes and run down her cheeks. He heard her sob of despair.

He grabbed her arm to stop her from leaving. His own anxiety tempered his words, along with his anger at her startling accusations. "What the hell are you talking about? What game?"

"Stop it, Wyatt! Just stop it!" She jerked her arm out of his grasp, making one last attempt to maintain control of the situation. "You know as well as I do exactly what I'm talking about—what you did to me fifteen years ago. Well, you're not going to get away with it this time."

His control had reached the limit. He grabbed her by the shoulders and held her firmly in his grasp. His angry words spewed out. "I don't know what the hell you're talking about!"

She could not keep it inside any longer. She glared at him through tear-filled eyes and blurted out what she'd held in check for so long. "Fifteen years ago you walked out on me. You took the coward's way, leaving while I was out of town for the weekend without so much as a word, not even a note saying goodbye. I came here, to this house. And in this very room your father informed me that you felt suffocated by me and couldn't stand it any longer. You had to have your space and your freedom and I was taking that away from you." A shudder moved through her body.

She gulped down a sob and continued before Wyatt could react to what she had said. She knew she had to say it all before he stopped her. "I was devastated. You couldn't have hurt me more if you had plunged a knife into my heart. I felt as if my entire existence had been jerked out from beneath me and I didn't know why. I managed to make a life for myself, but for all these years I've never understood exactly what I did to drive you away. And now, fifteen years later, you calmly stroll back into my life and act as if nothing happened and expect to pick things up right where we left off. Well, it's no good, Wyatt. I've tried to forgive and forget, but it's no good. I can't go on like this, pretending that it didn't exist!"

Wyatt's anger snapped into rage. He visibly trembled as he balled his hands into tight fists. His features contorted into an ominous mask of pure hatred. Vicki stepped back from him, totally unprepared for his reaction. She had never before seen that much rage come over someone so quickly.

Had she gone too far? Said too much? She knew as

soon as she let out her pent-up turmoil that it would be the end of any hope she might have held out for the future, but she had been unable to hold it inside for even one more second. A sudden feeling of loss engulfed her, but it was tempered with the knowledge that it was better for it to end now, like this, rather than later when her innocent son had become more involved.

Wyatt whirled around. His gaze charged about the room as if he were seeking out something specific. Then it settled on a large oil painting of Henry Edwards. He snatched it from the wall, clutching the ornate frame in both hands, and held it at arm's length in front of him. He glared at the portrait for a long moment, his face set in a expression of barely controlled fury.

He spit out harsh words, uttered with an undertone of dark malevolence. "You son of a bitch! Damn you! If you weren't already dead—" In a movement so quick that she did not see it coming, he hurled the painting across the room where it crashed into the opposite wall.

Then he turned toward Vicki. She shivered under the weight of his angry scowl and the rage that visibly coursed through his veins. She stumbled backward, her nerves shattered into a million pieces. Never in her wildest thoughts had she expected this reaction. She had never seen him so angry. Then his words cut through her again.

"And damn your father, too."

Eight

Wyatt wrapped his fingers around Vicki's wrist and pulled her to him. For a moment she felt truly frightened of what might happen. She felt the tension surge through his body, every one of his muscles hard and taut. His fingers threaded through her hair, then he cradled her head against his shoulder. Slowly, ever so slowly, the tension eased and his muscles relaxed. His words came out as a soft whisper.

"All these years wasted...fifteen years of my life taken from me...fifteen years in which we could have—" A shudder passed through his body, cutting off the rest of his words.

She tentatively reached her arms around his waist and returned his embrace. Her hurt and anger had been replaced with total confusion. She raised her head to look at him. Her question was hesitant, her words unsure. "I don't understand...what caused you to...why did you—"

"My father and your father...they could not have done a better job if they had actually formed an alliance and conspired to separate us." He placed a loving kiss on her forehead. Another shudder passed through him. "All those wasted years..."

"Your father and my father...what are you talking about?"

He took her hand and led her upstairs to his private suite. He seated her on the couch in the large alcove. "We're way past overdue in comparing notes, but at least now I understand why you refused to talk to me about it. All this time I considered myself to be the one who had been deserted and all the while..." He used his fingertips to still the words that started to form on her lips. "Let me tell you my version of what happened." He poured two glasses of wine, handed one of them to her, then turned and stared out the large bay window.

Wyatt took a calming breath, then a swallow from his wineglass. His words came out slowly at first. "You were gone for three days visiting that friend of yours who had gone out of state to college."

"Shirley."

"Yes, that's the one. Anyway, you left that morning. About three o'clock that afternoon my father came in to me, all upset about an emergency situation at the South American mining operation. He said I had to go immediately, that millions of dollars were at stake. The next morning I was on my way to Brazil. On the way out of town I stopped at the market and gave your father a letter to give to you explaining what had happened and that I didn't know how long I'd be gone. I didn't even know if I would be anyplace where I'd be able to contact you directly. Then one of my father's employees drove me to San Francisco so I could catch a flight."

Vicki started to say something, but he quickly stopped her. "Please, let me finish." He took another sip from his wineglass. "I was gone for two months. The only communication I had with the outside world was through our San Francisco corporate headquarters. I sent several letters to you via the air-freight pouch, but I never got anything from you in return.

"When I finally got home, I went directly to your house. Your father informed me that you had moved away and didn't want me bothering you. He refused to tell me where you'd gone. I asked my father and he said he heard that you had gotten married, then added that I was well rid of you. I didn't know what to think or what to believe. All I knew was that you had not answered any of my letters, you had moved away and had made no attempt to contact me."

He continued to stare out the window at nothing in particular. "I think I actually hated you for a while...or at least I tried to. For fifteen years I've just gone through the motions of living and working, not really caring about much of anything. The globe-trotting, the world of international business, the social whirl—all of it left me empty inside. I even got engaged for a while, but I knew I could never go through with the wedding.

"Then one day I decided to return to Sea Cliff, although I'm not exactly sure why. I walked into the market and there you were. I was elated and angry all at the same time. I wanted to make you as miserable as I had been, but when I found out that your father had just died and about how you lost your husband, I didn't know what to do.

"I did manage to get one clear thought to jell inside me. It was a second chance for us to be together and I wasn't going to let it get away. I immediately knew one thing above all else. I had to find out why you left, but every time I tried to talk about it you cut me off."

He finally turned to face her and was immediately captured by the sight of her tearstained cheeks. Then he saw the soft glow of acceptance in her eyes. It was as if everything bad had suddenly been swept away and the world was new again.

"Oh, Wyatt..." She held her hand out to him. He took it, helped her to her feet, then folded her into the warmth of his arms. "I've been so frightened and so confused ever since I heard you were moving back to Sea Cliff. For fifteen years I couldn't figure out what it was I had done to drive you away. Your father said I had been smothering you, demanding too much attention. I searched through every memory I held of the time we spent together, trying to find some clue to what I'd done, some hint of what had gone wrong. Each and every time I came up blank.

"And then, when you acted as if nothing had happened, I didn't know what to do or think. I couldn't figure out why you kept wanting to bring up the past, to dredge up all those painful memories I thought I had safely tucked away where they couldn't hurt me. I was so afraid of history repeating itself. I had lost you once. Then I had lost my husband. I didn't think I would be able to handle that type of emotional up- heaval a third time if you decided you needed more space and freedom, just as I thought you had done before.''

She felt his arms close tighter around her. For the first time since she had heard about Wyatt returning to Sea Cliff, she felt as if everything would be all right. Well, almost everything...at least for the moment. There was still her son—*their* son. What was best for Richie had to come ahead of her own needs and desires. Somehow she had to find a way to make everything work out. But how?

All her thoughts vanished the instant his mouth covered hers. In one very heated moment all the passion of their youth was unleashed with an incendiary fury that threatened to set the room on fire. She slipped her hands beneath his sweater and ran them up his bare back. He was all she had ever wanted and now it looked as if there might be a future for them after all.

His lips brushed across her cheek, then he whispered in her ear, ''Dinner is already prepared. It's downstairs in the kitchen. All we have to do is warm it in the oven.'' His voice had turned thick with the need coursing through his body. He kissed the tender spot behind her ear.

She allowed a sly grin to turn the corners of her mouth. ''Maybe we should work up an appetite first.''

''I already have a raging appetite and there's nothing in the kitchen that's going to satisfy it.''

That ended the conversation. Wyatt swept her up in his arms and carried her over to his king-size bed, lowering her to her feet in front of the nightstand. One by one he unfastened the buttons of her blouse until it fell open, exposing the lacy fabric of her bra. He slipped his hands inside her blouse, ran them up her rib cage, then caressed the outside edge of her breasts.

Her bra hooks were in front. A moment later he had them unfastened.

Vicki shrugged out of her blouse and bra at the same time. While she did that, Wyatt pulled off his sweater. The articles of clothing fell to the floor. A minute later they had both divested themselves of the rest of their clothes. He lowered her to the softness of the large bed, then stretched out beside her.

Bare skin touched bare skin along the length of their bodies. A shiver of delight puckered her nipples into taut peaks. She ran her foot along the edge of his calf and her hand across his chest.

He wrapped his arms around her and pulled her body tightly against his. Then his mouth found hers. He thrust his tongue between her lips, reveling in the texture and taste he found there. He felt as if an incredible weight had been lifted from his shoulders. For the first time in fifteen years he knew happiness. For the first time in fifteen years he looked forward to what the future held for him...for Vicki and him.

He cupped the underside of her breast in his hand, then lowered his head and drew her nipple into his mouth. Her soft murmur of pleasure reinforced his physical need as well as his emotional desires. Her skin evoked the texture of the smoothest satin. Her hair emulated strands of fine silk. Her intoxicating taste set his heart pounding and took his breath away. He lost himself totally in the sensuality of Vicki Bingham.

The moment his mouth closed around her nipple Vicki sank into a swirl of hedonistic delight. She wanted Wyatt Edwards—the feel of his mouth, the texture of his tongue, his hardened sex deep inside her. She wanted him, all of him, and she wanted him now.

He reached for the drawer in the nightstand and withdrew a packet. A moment later he nudged her thigh aside then smoothly thrust his rigid length into the depth of her womanhood.

Time did not exist for them. Arms, legs, hands, mouths, lips, tongues—they tasted, touched, indulged every facet of tactile pleasure, and all the while their hips moved together in harmonious ecstasy. The very essence of their existence flowed together to create a complete union of body and soul.

Finally, with their passions momentarily spent, they lay in each other's arms, basking in the afterglow of their intense lovemaking. She placed a soft kiss against his chest, then ran her fingers through the wisps of damp chest hair. He traced the curve of her breast with his fingertip.

Wyatt rolled her body over on top of him, slid his hand down the smoothness of her back, then cupped the curve of her bottom. "Stay all night with me. I want to make love to you in every room of this house—and then on the patio just as dawn ushers in a new day." His words floated sensually across her awareness.

The huskiness of her voice matched his. "This is a very large house with lots of rooms."

"That's right. It could take days, maybe even weeks, to get to all the rooms. Then we could start at the beginning and do it again."

"Mmm…" It was the soft moan of a contented woman who liked what she was hearing.

"And then maybe along the way—" he smoothed her hair away from her face "—we can work on creating a new life…a baby." He placed a tender kiss on her forehead. "I want very much to have a family...for us to be a family."

His words shocked her, causing her to wince. "A baby?" A sick feeling settled in the pit of her stomach. She could not stop the quaver in her voice. "No...no—that's not possible."

"I didn't mean right now. I meant...maybe...well, sometime in the near future. I just thought that we..." Her response had been so quick and emphatic that he suddenly felt very uneasy about having blurted out what was on his mind.

"Now...later...it doesn't matter. I...well, I can't have any more children." The sorrow began working its way to her consciousness. "I almost miscarried Richie on two separate occasions. The doctor told me no more children."

He cradled her head against his chest. "I'm sorry. I didn't mean to intrude..." His voice was very soft, reflecting the sadness that had begun to take hold of him. He wished he had not brought up children, regardless of how much they had been on his mind. Maybe he needed to slow down, to put less emphasis on the future as a means of recapturing the lost past. For right now perhaps the best thing would be to simply concentrate on the present and let the future take care of itself. After all, the major problem had been resolved. Everything else would fall into place naturally.

He nestled her hips against his, the moist heat of her sex radiating to his manhood. He kissed her tenderly on the lips, then held her tightly in his embrace. "How about it, Vicki? We can start all over again. Clean slate, as if the past fifteen years never existed. This time there won't be any obstacles."

If only that was true, Vicki thought. They might have resolved fifteen years of anger, hurt and resentment between them, but there was still an obstacle—a very real obstacle—and his name was Richie. She knew she was probably a little too protective of her son, but she could not help it. He was the only child she would ever have and he had already been handed too many bad turns in his young life. She knew for certain that she could not walk up to her son and say, *Guess what? Wyatt is your real father.*

Wyatt felt her body stiffen in his arms and saw the worried look that clouded her features. He brushed her hair away from her face and gazed into her eyes. A new fear had settled there, or maybe an old fear had resurfaced. He placed a loving kiss on her lips.

"What's the matter, Vicki? I thought we had everything out in the open at long last, all the problems of the past washed away. Is there...is there something else?"

She laid her head against his shoulder and placed her hand on his chest. His strong heartbeat resonated to her fingertips. There was a silent strength about him, a confidence that made her wonder, if only for a fleeting moment, whether she could tell him the truth about their son. Part of her wanted to, if only for her own selfish reasons, but the logical portion of her consciousness prevailed.

"No...nothing else." She snuggled more comfortably inside his embrace. "I just never thought I would ever see you again, let alone fifteen years later. And I certainly never imagined we would end up making love like this." She felt his arms tighten around her, drawing her more protectively against his body.

"It's all been such a shock. I guess I'm just beginning to fully comprehend the impact of events—both fifteen years ago and now.'' Even more important than the events themselves was what to do about them and what they meant for the future. How could she juggle her feelings for Wyatt with her need to protect her son?

She contemplated the possibility of actually having an ongoing relationship with Wyatt. Then another thought occurred to her. Just what were his true feelings for her? Fifteen years ago they had never talked about being in love. And now Wyatt had gone so far as to say he wanted them to have a baby. But at no time had he ever mentioned love or marriage.

They had certainly recaptured the passion of their youth, but could there really be more than stolen moments of lovemaking? If only some divine inspiration would strike her, something that would tell her how to handle the balance between the two men in her life.

Wyatt continued to hold Vicki in his arms, but the mood had changed from heated passion to quiet reflection. They each seemed to be lost in their own thoughts.

He was not sure what to think. Vicki had given his life meaning once again. She was everything he had ever wanted. And her son—he had been surprised that she had a son, but he should not have been. After all, she had been married. A moment of sorrow intruded into his thoughts. He had wanted her children to be his, not some other man's.

He became reflective again as he thought about Vicki's son. Richie was a great kid, just the kind of son he would like to have. She had done an excellent job of raising him, especially in light of the fact that for the last five years she had done it alone. He felt sure Richie's father would be proud of the fine young man he had turned into.

The bad times had finally been put to rest, but something was still wrong. Vicki was hiding something from him—something that made her sad. He wanted so much to know what it was, to help her conquer the anguish that continued to gnaw at her.

He placed a tender kiss on her cheek. "You never answered me."

"Which question?" Sudden anxiety settled in the pit of her stomach.

He kissed her shoulder, then nuzzled the side of her neck. "Let's start with the one where I asked you to spend the night and work our way up to starting our life over again."

"Spending the night? *All* night?"

"Yes, *all* night. I want to wake up with you by my side." He found her mouth before she could answer him.

Vicki stood at the alcove window in Wyatt's bedroom and stared out across the moonlit landscape. She glanced back toward the bed to verify that he was still asleep. The distant bonging from the grandfather clock downstairs in the living room sounded as forlorn as she felt. Four o'clock in the morning, and she had only managed to doze off in brief snatches.

As much as she truly loved Wyatt, she feared for her son's well-being even more. She also feared what would happen if Wyatt ever discovered her secret. Would he understand, or would he hate her for keeping it from him? Would he accept Richie as his own, or resent him?

And what about Richie? Would he accept Wyatt?

And more importantly, would her son forgive *her?* The tears spilled over and ran down her cheeks. How was it possible to be so happy and so miserable at the same time? She quickly brushed the tears away and returned to bed, trying her best to slide in under the covers without disturbing Wyatt.

He turned over on his side, reached out to place his arm around her waist, and pulled her body close to his. He nuzzled his face into her hair. A soft moan— more of a low, sexy growl—escaped his throat. She could not tell if he was asleep or awake, but either way she felt so safe and comfortable in his embrace. She closed her eyes and finally drifted off to sleep, but her dreams were troubled.

She did not know how long she had been sleeping when she woke to the gentle touch on her shoulder. She rolled over, opened her eyes, and was greeted by the sight of Wyatt holding a breakfast tray. The tantalizing aroma of freshly brewed coffee filled the air. She sat up and ran her fingers through her tousled hair.

"Good morning." Wyatt set the tray on the nightstand.

"Mmm, that coffee smells great." She studied the items on the tray for a moment. "I'm famished." She lowered her gaze as a hint of embarrassment swept over her. "We never did get around to dinner last night."

He sat down on the edge of the bed next to her. His voice was soft, seductive and very persuasive. "I guess my hosting skills need some work. I invited you for dinner, then never let you get near the food." He leaned over and placed a kiss behind her ear while trailing his fingers across the swell of her breast.

That marvelously sexy smile of his sent little shivers across the surface of her skin, followed by trails of heat in the wake of his touch. She returned his smile. "No need to apologize. I can assure you I didn't mind one bit."

His expression turned serious as he cupped her chin in his hand. "All those years, Vicki. All that time lost."

She averted her eyes. It had not been lost time, not totally. It was true that Wyatt Edwards was the one overwhelming, passionate love of her life, but Robert Bingham had loved her and had made a happy home for Richie and her. The three of them had been a family. They were years she could not simply dismiss. She picked up her cup from the tray and swallowed her regrets along with the coffee.

Setting the empty cup on the tray, she swung her legs over the side of the bed. "I'd better get dressed."

Wyatt playfully shoved her back on the bed and covered her body with his. "No need to reach for your clothes on my account," he teased as a wry grin tugged at the corners of his mouth.

She gently pushed him away. "Well, it isn't exactly on your account. I need to get to work. We don't open until ten o'clock on Sunday morning, but by the time I get home, take care of some personal business, then shower and change clothes, I'll barely make it in time."

He ran his fingers through her hair, followed by a brief kiss. "Can't you call Noreen and ask her to work today?"

"No..." She rose to her feet. His nearness was far too tempting. She could not deny that where Wyatt was concerned she had very little willpower or self-control. "Today is Noreen's mother's birthday. She's taking her out to lunch, then to a movie." Grabbing her clothes from where they had fallen to the floor, she hurried toward the bathroom. "I really need to be going."

"I thought maybe we could have breakfast on the patio and..." They were wasted words that bounced off the closed bathroom door. The rest of his sentence was reduced to a mere whisper. "And then talk about us, and our future together."

Wyatt sank into a chair, his mind clouded with confusion over what had just taken place. Every time he thought the problems of the past had been worked out, something new happened. Once again they had spent a fantastic night making love and the next morning it was as if they were back at square one. Once again she seemed to be shutting him out of her life as firmly as she had shut the bathroom door.

Vicki emerged from the bathroom a few minutes later. She had dressed, run a comb through her hair and put on a hint of lipstick. She seemed nervous. Even her movements were edgy. He stopped her before she could get her car keys out of her purse and led her over to the couch in the alcove.

"We have to talk, Vicki. We need to make plans."

She nervously bit at her lip. "Not now, Wyatt."

"Then when?"

"I...I don't know. There are too many other considerations—"

He grew impatient with the way she kept trying to shove him aside. "What other considerations?"

Vicki rose from the couch, took a calming breath, then spoke with what she hoped was confidence and control. "I have a son to consider…a son who has already had too many upheavals in his life."

She did not wait for a response, but quickly left the house. The turmoil twisted in her stomach as she drove down the hill. They might have resolved what happened fifteen years ago, but things were still very unsettled between them. Now, even more than before, she agonized over whether she should tell Wyatt about Richie. She also worried about how she could possibly explain the truth to her son. Things were definitely far from being settled.

Wyatt watched from the alcove window as she drove through the front gates. He felt lost, not sure about what to do or where to turn. He ended up wandering out to the stables. Maybe a brisk ride.

"Mornin', Wyatt." Fred stood in the doorway of the tack room.

"Good morning, Fred. I think I'll go out for a ride." He started for the tack room, but Fred did not move out of his way.

The man nervously shifted his weight from one foot to the other. Wyatt looked at him curiously. "Is something the matter?"

"That…uh…was Vicki Bingham who just left here, wasn't it?"

Wyatt eyed him suspiciously, carefully measuring his words. "Is there some point you're trying to make?"

"Well…I don't hold none with gossip, but I heard somethin' yesterday. Alice Thackery and me was passing a few minutes in conversation…" Fred paused, as if reconsidering what he was about to say.

A little tickle of caution started up inside Wyatt.

The image of Alice staring at him, then at Richie, and back at him again leapt to his mind. "And?"

"Well, now…we all know what a terrible busybody Alice is, but I thought since she was talkin' about you—"

"Me? What in the world could that miserable old crone have to say about me?" The tickle of caution turned into all-out wariness when he noticed Fred's obvious discomfort.

"Well, it ain't just you…" Fred glanced down at the ground as if gathering his thoughts. "It's…uh…"

Wyatt's nerves were already tightly strung. He did not have the time or the desire for a game of cat and mouse. "It's *what?*"

Fred looked up at him again. "It's about you and Vicki…"

The anxiety churning inside him began to subside. "What could she possibly be saying about Vicki and me that wouldn't be common knowledge? We have been seen together on numerous occasions since I moved back."

"It's more about you…and her son."

The anxiety returned in full force, but Wyatt was not sure exactly why. "Richie and me?" He fixed Fred with a hard look. "What about us?"

"Well, the talk is that Vicki was pregnant before she moved away and…well, that would mean her son—"

"Oh, my God!" Reality struck Wyatt like a bolt of lightning out of a clear blue sky. He could not stop the stunned expression that he knew covered his face. It matched the shock that jolted through his consciousness and the tremor that shook his body.

He whirled around and started back toward the

house. His pace quickened until he broke into a full run. His boots pounded against the steps and across the porch. He slammed through the door, raced up the stairs and into his room.

Richie was his son, his own flesh and blood.

Every fiber of his existence told him it was the truth. And Vicki had purposely kept the knowledge from him.

His chest heaved in anger. Even when he had mentioned his longing to have a family, a perfect opening for her to tell him they already had a child, she still had not told him about Richie.

How could she have done this to him? How? A burning rage ignited inside him. They would have this out right now.

He grabbed the phone and started to dial her number. He gripped the receiver so tightly his knuckles turned white. No, this was far too important to handle over the phone. He needed to see her in person, confront her face-to-face. He slammed the receiver into the cradle, grabbed his car keys and started for the door. Then logic and reason finally got control of his emotions.

He stopped in the doorway, leaned his forehead against the frame, and took several calming breaths before turning back toward his desk. If yesterday's revelations had done nothing else, they should have given him some insight into how to handle this situation. Fifteen years of his life had been thrown away because his father and Vicki's father told him something and he had accepted it as the truth without making any attempt to verify it on his own. He would not make that mistake again.

Alice Thackery was a gossipy, mean-spirited busybody. There was no reason to believe that what she had said was anything more than her own malicious and petty invention. If he confronted Vicki with this and it proved not to be true—well, he preferred not to contemplate just how much damage it could do to the relationship he was desperately trying to reestablish. Calmer heads needed to prevail.

He picked up the phone again and instead of calling Vicki he dialed his attorney in San Francisco. He waited impatiently. George Weston finally answered on the fourth ring.

"George, it's Wyatt. Sorry to bother you at home on a Sunday morning, but I need some information and I need it immediately. I want to know the date of the marriage of Victoria Dalton and Robert Bingham and the exact date of the birth of her son. His name is Richie. I assume that's short for Richard. We're talking between fourteen and fifteen years ago, probably in Dallas, Texas. And, George—this is personal and highly confidential."

George sounded slightly confused. "Sure, Wyatt. I'll put someone on it first thing in the morning. Unless there's some sort of problem, I should have some information for you by Monday afternoon or Tuesday morning."

"Well, make it as fast as you can. Fax the information to me at home. I'd also like a copy of the marriage certificate and birth certificate if that can be arranged."

Was it possible? Wyatt stared out the alcove window. Could Richie be his son? His son. The thought caused a warm feeling to settle inside him—a warm feeling quickly supplanted by a resurgence of the anger just beneath it.

On two separate weekends he and Vicki had made love with all the passion that two people could possibly share. There had been ample opportunity for her to tell him the truth, and she had chosen not to say anything. He told himself to calm down as he turned away from the window. He would wait for George Weston's report before taking any action. That meant he had to stay away from Vicki until then. He could not handle the uncertainty of being around her or Richie and not knowing if the boy was his son.

He took a deep breath, then congratulated himself on how well he was handling things. Anger did not accomplish anything. He even managed to rationalize why Vicki had not told him about his son. After all, up until last night she honestly believed that he had walked out on her.

But this morning was another story. He felt the anger building inside him again…along with a sinking feeling of despair and helplessness.

Vicki spent a busy day at the market. Business was especially brisk for a Sunday, for which she was very thankful. She did not want time on her hands. She did not want to have to think about… Well, just to think— period.

She glanced at the clock, noting that the workday was finally at an end. She put the Closed sign in the window and locked the door, then hurried home. Richie would be back from his camping trip any minute and she knew he would be hungry. She started dinner, and tried to block the fears threatening to engulf her. She needed to present a calm outward appearance for her son.

About an hour later Richie came in the door carrying his sleeping bag and the duffel bag with his clothes. He dropped them noisily on the floor, then stood defiantly staring at her. His body language sent out silent signals that immediately tied her insides into tightly drawn knots.

"Richie? What's the matter?"

The scowl that covered his face made it seem as if he were deciding whether or not to say anything at all, rather than deciding exactly what he was going to say. When he finally spoke, his words were irate, but he was unable to hide the hint of uncertainty that churned just beneath the surface.

"What's going on between you and Wyatt?"

She tried to swallow the solid lump of fear his question had produced. "What are you talking about?"

"Did he spend the night here last weekend? Did he?" His expression became even more defiant.

"What? What do you mean?" Her words came out in a shocked rush as her eyes widened in surprise. This was not what she had expected.

Richie repeated the words slowly and emphatically. "Did he stay here all night, or didn't he? It was a simple question…either yes he did or no he didn't."

Vicki's insides knotted into a hard ball. She couldn't ignore her son's question, but she knew that the truth would only make the situation worse.

And she couldn't help but feel that a "yes" answer would change all their lives forever.

Nine

Vicki swallowed a couple of times as she frantically searched for just the right thing to say in answer to Richie's very definite accusation. She took a calming breath, straightened her posture and brought forth her most official mother-of-a-teenager voice. "I don't believe I care for your attitude, young man. Why would you ask such a thing?"

Richie did not physically back down, but she was relieved to see the aggressiveness drain from his manner. "I...uh...overheard a couple of the guys talking about it last night. I guess they thought I was sleepin'." A hint of embarrassment flashed across his face and he quickly glanced down at the floor.

"Oh, really?" Her fear was replaced by irritation that she should have been the subject of adolescent gossip. "And just where did a couple of teenage boys get all this information?"

"Well…" Richie was becoming less and less secure in his position. "I think they said they heard old lady Thackery telling it to someone."

"Humph! Alice Thackery again. Well, consider the source, young man. That should have told you all you needed to know. This is the same Alice Thackery who told me you almost ran her down with your bike."

"Well, yeah…but—"

Her manner softened a little as she tried to address her son's concerns. "It's true that Wyatt was here that night. We had dinner and talked about…well, talked about the past. He did stay pretty late. Maybe someone saw his car here and just assumed…"

Deeper and deeper. It could never be just one little lie. That lie required another lie to go with it, then another and another. She was digging a bottomless hole. "Anyway, that's all there was to it. Now—" she gestured toward the kitchen in a desperate attempt to change the subject "—how about something to eat? You put your things away and I'll get dinner on the table."

Richie hesitated for a minute, as if he still had more to say, but finally grabbed his belongings and went to his room. Vicki breathed a sigh of relief. She had handled that particular confrontation, but she knew it would not be the last one. She had known Alice Thackery was going to cause problems, and she had been right.

She put dinner on the table while Richie put his things away. A myriad of thoughts circulated through her mind. If she were to confide things… Sadly, she shook her head. Now it was *if*, where just a day or two ago it had been *never*. She knew she was just kidding herself if she continued to think she could keep her secret forever. But how could she tell those involved and still keep everything together? How could she tell Wyatt without driving him away? And how could she tell Richie without him ending up resenting Wyatt and hating her?

It seemed to be an insurmountable problem. She did not even know whom she should tell first. Should she discuss it with Richie and risk an immature outburst reaching Wyatt's ears before she was ready to tell him? Or should she tell Wyatt first and hope he would understand and join with her in presenting Richie with the facts?

She could try to continue keeping her secret hidden under an ever-increasing pile of lies, knowing full well that either Wyatt or Richie could find out on their own at any time. Her alternative was confessing the truth to the two people who mattered most to her and letting the chips fall where they may. Either way, she risked losing both of them forever. No matter how she played it out in her mind, it always ended up the same. It was a no-win situation for everyone concerned—especially for her.

Richie returned to the kitchen and took his place at the table. He did not say anything. He simply sat there and stared at her. Vicki suddenly felt very uncomfortable. For the first time in her life her son's presence created an awkward chill inside her. There was no doubt in her mind that he had more questions than the one he had already asked. She avoided his look by pretending to be concerned about the placement of the silverware on the table.

Finally the silence grew too loud for her to handle. She nervously cleared her throat. "What all did you do on your camp-out this weekend? Did you have a good time?''

"Yeah, we had a good time." He offered no additional information.

"What did you do? Did you go hiking? Fishing? How was the weather? Did you encounter any wild animals?" She could hear her fear in her words, in the continuous string of questions.

Richie scrunched his face into a frown as he continued to stare at her. "What's the matter with you?"

"Nothing's the matter with me. Why do you ask?" She nervously bit at her lower lip as her gaze darted erratically around the room.

"Because you're acting weird. You rearranged all the silverware on the table. You took two helpings of green beans and ignored the salad, then you put salad dressing on the green beans. Isn't that a good enough reason to ask what's wrong?"

Vicki looked at her dinner plate. She was not even aware of what she had done. "I…uh…" Anxiety churned her stomach to the point where she thought for a moment that she might actually throw up. She shoved her dinner plate away and stood up. "I…I'm not feeling very well. I think I might be coming down with the flu…" Her voice trailed off as she ran out of words. "Or something."

"Yeah…right." He eyed her suspiciously. His tone of voice said he clearly did not believe her explanation.

She tried to regain the control she felt slipping away. "Now listen here, young man. I won't tolerate that sarcastic—"

She turned and quickly left the kitchen. She could not believe how far she had sunk into her self-made quagmire. She had actually started to chastise her son for not believing the lie she had just told. What in the world did she think she was trying to do? What could possibly be gained from perpetuating the myth she had built? Maybe the thing to do would be to sell the business, then she and Richie could move back to Dallas. At least there no one would be gossiping about the past. And she would not have to face Wyatt, knowing she was denying him the family he wanted and deserved.

She went to the glassed-in porch, sat in the corner of the couch and stared out across the yard. Tears trickled down her cheeks and she made no attempt to stop them. Sooner or later it would all come out and the longer she waited the more difficult it would be.

"I think you and Wyatt have something going now. I think you had something going when you lived here before and not just this 'We might have gone to the movies once or twice' junk that you both tried to tell me."

Vicki jumped at the sound of her son's voice. She had not heard him come to the door. She quickly rubbed her hands across her eyes and cheeks in an effort to wipe away the tears before facing him.

"And I think whatever it was that happened between you two before was why you left here and it's what you fight about now."

Vicki took a deep breath and tried to gain some composure and courage. "What in the world would make you say such a thing?"

"I got two eyes and two ears. I can see and I can hear. Were you in love with him? Are you in love with him now?"

Her son was, indeed, no longer a boy. He stood in

front of her, trying his best to deal with an adult situation by being very straightforward and matter-of-fact. She could see the uncertainty in his eyes, but his voice and actions showed no indecision.

"Oh, Richie..." Her sigh of resignation filled the air. Once again the tears ran silently down her cheeks. She reached out and smoothed his hair away from his forehead, then cupped his chin in her hand. This time he did not brush her hand away or shoot her a look of irritation. "When did you stop being my little boy and turn into such a mature young man?" But was he mature enough to handle the truth...all of it?

"Ever since I overheard the guys talking about what old lady Thackery said I've been giving it a lot of thought. And...well...I know kids at school who live with their mothers. For most of them, it's because their parents are divorced, but for a couple of them it's because their dads died. And...well, some of them...well, their mothers got married again and they say it's okay. Of course, most of them still have their real dad around and still see him. And...well..."

It was obvious that Richie was becoming very nervous and self-conscious about what he was trying to say. Vicki's heart went out to him. She so much wanted to pull him into her arms and help him, but she knew it was not what he wanted. He was attempting to handle the situation, or at least his perception of it, as an adult. He had thought out the problem in a mature manner, had arrived at a conclusion and now he was trying to share it with her. She waited quietly for him to collect his thoughts and form his words.

Besides, she was afraid to volunteer even the slightest hint of information for fear she might reveal too much or start him thinking in a direction he had not considered. She would wait until she heard exactly where he was going with this, what he suspected and how he had decided to deal with it.

"Well, it seems to me that if you and Wyatt hadn't had some kind of fight that you would have stayed here and probably gotten married instead of moving to Dallas and meeting Dad. So, I figured that's what you guys are fighting about…that and what to do about me. And…well, you're not getting any younger and you're going to need someone to take care of you when I go off to college. So, if you and Wyatt want to get married, then it's okay with me."

Now the tears really streamed down her cheeks. "Oh, Richie…" She reached out and pulled him into her arms. He had put together bits and pieces and come up with some correct answers, as far as his puzzle pieces allowed. "I love you, honey. You are, without a doubt, the most important person in my life." She could not contain the laugh that forced its way out. "In spite of that crack about my not getting any younger."

She released him and indicated the sofa cushion next to her. "Here, sit down." She waited a moment until Richie got comfortable. "Oddly enough, it was just yesterday that Wyatt and I were able to put the pieces of this story together ourselves so that we knew exactly what really happened all those years ago. It seems that my father and Wyatt's father both have a lot to answer for."

Vicki explained to her son what had happened, what it was that she and Wyatt had finally discovered to be the truth. All of it, that is, except the part about her being pregnant. With everything else coming out in the open the way it had and with Richie having already given it considerable thought, it looked as if she would never have to disclose Richie's true parentage. She breathed an inner sigh of relief. There was light at the end of the tunnel.

Richie sat quietly for a while, obviously turning over in his mind what she had told him. Finally he looked up at her. "So, does this mean that you and Wyatt are going to get married now?"

"I'm afraid that's a little presumptuous on your part. Wyatt and I have never discussed marriage." A sadness overtook her, tingeing her words with a hint of sorrow. "Or love. Not back then and not now." The light at the end of the tunnel began to fade again. At no time had Wyatt ever said he loved her and he had certainly never even hinted at the possibility of marriage. He had talked about having a family, but not about marriage. Once again uncertainty blanketed her future.

It was time to change the subject, and Richie seemed ready, even relieved to do just that.

She forced an upbeat attitude. "Have you finished your dinner?"

Wyatt did not have any appetite for dinner. He had spent the last two hours pacing up and down in front of his fax machine, as if that would force the machine to spit something out. Finally he was rewarded by the sound that signaled an incoming fax. He watched as the sheets of paper were ejected from the machine. There were two items clipped from a newspaper, followed by a one-page memo from George Weston.

He continued to stare at the papers without touching them. He was afraid to pick them up, afraid of what they might say. He was not even sure what he wanted them to say. His hand trembled as he removed the sheets from the tray where they had fallen.

The first newspaper clipping was the announcement of the wedding of Robert Bingham and Victoria Dalton. He noted the date of the marriage. He did not know exactly how old Richie was to the month, but one thing was startlingly clear—she had to have been pregnant at the time she married. But just how pregnant was she? Was she far enough along for the baby to have been conceived before she left Sea Cliff? The other clipping was the birth announcement of a son, Richard Bingham. Wyatt squinted and stared, then reached for a magnifying glass. But the date of Richie's birth was too smeared to read.

He grabbed George Weston's memo and quickly scanned it, hoping it would provide the missing information. A moment later he set it aside in frustration. It did not shed any light on the problem. It merely said George could not obtain copies of the wedding certificate and birth certificate until the following day when the appropriate state offices would be open. He said he would fax them as soon as possible.

Impatience gnawed at Wyatt's insides. There would be one more day of waiting before he had an answer.

If the birth certificate showed that Richie was born too late to have been conceived that night at the beach, then it meant Richie was not his son. It also meant that Vicki had not kept a secret of this magnitude from him. It meant one more thing, too. He and Vicki would never have any children of their own.

If Richie's birth certificate showed that the boy was conceived before Wyatt left for South America, then it meant Richie was his child. He and Vicki might not be able to have any more children of their own, but they did have a son.

A dark scowl spread across his face, and he clenched his jaw in anger. It also meant that Vicki had purposely denied him his child.

"Hello." Wyatt grabbed the phone on the first ring.

"Wyatt? It's Richie...Richie Bingham."

"Richie?" He had been expecting a call from George Weston. He had not received the certificates George had promised yesterday and had grown more and more impatient with each passing minute. Richie was the last person he expected to hear from.

"Well, this is certainly a surprise." A sudden jolt of panic hit him. "Is there something wrong? Is Vicki okay?"

"Mom's fine. I...uh—" Richie nervously cleared his throat. "I believe we have something that needs to be discussed. Could you pick me up from school?"

Be careful...keep calm until you find out what he wants. That was the first thought that occurred to Wyatt. "Well...yes, I could do that, Richie. Are you ready to go now?"

"Yeah, I'll meet you at the front entrance."

Wyatt did not want to leave his office until he had received the certificate copies from George Weston. However, what Richie wanted to talk about was obviously something very important to the boy even though it made Wyatt extremely nervous. There was something about Richie's voice that gave added emphasis to his words and compelled Wyatt to agree.

He checked the fax machine again, turned on his telephone answering machine, grabbed his keys from the desk and left the house. He drove straight to the school and immediately spotted Richie waiting by the door. Richie ran to his car and climbed in the front seat.

"I was certainly surprised to get your call," Wyatt said, feeling an uncomfortable twinge as he observed Richie's serious expression. "What is it you wanted to discuss with me?"

Richie turned toward Wyatt and squared his shoulders. The boy seemed to study him for a moment before speaking. "Perhaps we could go somewhere else other than the driveway in front of the school? I don't want anybody to see us talking. This is a personal discussion that's no one else's business."

The twinge increased to a definite feeling of discomfort. "Sure...uh, do you want to go back to my house or would you rather go to your house?"

"No!" Richie leaned back in the seat, seeming to calm his outburst. "No, I don't want to go home. Maybe your house would be best."

"Okay." Wyatt attempted to quell his mounting apprehension as he drove back to his place. They rode along in silence, and Wyatt sneaked sporadic sidelong glances at Richie. He could see the boy's obvious nervousness and occasional flashes of uncertainty.

They pulled up in front of the house and got out of the car. Wyatt's anxiety had increased tenfold since leaving the school. "Do you want to go inside the house or would you rather take a walk down by the stables?"

"Uh...well..." Richie's expression was uncertain.

Wyatt made the decision for him. "Why don't we go into the kitchen? We can have something to eat while we talk."

"Uh...yeah...that's fine."

Wyatt grabbed a beer for himself and a soft drink for Richie, then took a bag of chips from the cupboard. As soon as they were settled on the stools at the breakfast bar, Wyatt fixed Richie with a quizzical gaze. "Well? What is it you wanted to discuss?"

Richie nervously cleared his throat, set his soft-drink can on the counter, then looked up at Wyatt. "I want to know what your intentions are toward my mother."

Wyatt nearly choked on his swallow of beer. He felt the shock cover his face, but he could not stop it. "You want to know…what?"

Richie repeated his statement, this time with much greater conviction. "I want to know what your intentions are toward my mother. Do you plan to marry her?"

Wyatt was clearly at a loss for words. "I…uh, well…what makes you think Vicki and I even have that kind of a relationship?"

A hint of irritation flashed across Richie's face and settled in his voice. "Why does everyone insist on treating me like a kid? Why can't you just answer my question?"

"Well…you do have to admit that it's not your run-of-the-mill question. I was just trying to figure out why you would have asked it, that's all."

"I've watched the two of you and I've listened to the way you guys argue. I knew something was going on between you. Last night Mom told me about everything and how you two just figured out what happened a long time ago. So I want to know what you plan to do now."

"Just exactly what did she tell you?" Wyatt knew he needed to be very cautious. He did not want to say anything that would contradict whatever Vicki had told her son.

Richie let out an exasperated sigh, clearly showing that he was tired of covering the same ground again. He quickly repeated what Vicki had told him about the events of fifteen years ago. "So does that agree with your version of what happened?" he said, an edge of sarcasm in his voice.

"Yes, it does," Wyatt answered without hesitation. Vicki had told Richie exactly what they had figured out Saturday evening.

"So maybe we can get back to my original question. What happens now? What are your intentions?"

"I don't know, Richie. It's not that simple. Vicki and I have other things we need to talk about." As soon as the words were out of his mouth, he wished he had not said them. The entire conversation had him very unnerved and he had spoken without thinking.

Richie took a sip of his soft drink. "Yeah...right." Then he took a large swallow as he turned away from Wyatt and looked out the kitchen window.

Richie's words, his tone of voice, his body language—everything about the boy told Wyatt he was not satisfied with that answer. But Wyatt did not know what else to tell him. Until he had satisfied himself about whether or not he was Richie's father, he could not give further consideration to answering Richie's question. He did not know how confirmation of that information might change things. Besides...he did not know the answer. He had thought he knew what he wanted, but now he was not sure of anything. And he certainly did not know what Vicki wanted for the future.

Wyatt tried to reassure Richie. "Look...I can understand your being apprehensive about so many changes in your life. Maybe even the added problem of hearing…'' He thought about his conversation with Fred, about Alice Thackery's indiscriminate tongue-wagging, and about how her nasty sniping could just as easily have reached Richie's ears. ''Maybe you've heard some idle town gossip. But, I can honestly tell you that Vicki and I have not made any plans. If we do, then we will both make sure you know before anyone else does.'' Wyatt offered an encouraging smile. ''Does that meet with your approval?'' A second later he realized he was holding his breath while waiting for Richie's response.

Richie took another swallow of his soft drink, grabbed a handful of chips, then turned around to face Wyatt. He stared at him for a moment before answering. ''Yeah, I guess it does…for now.''

Wyatt did not have any difficulty grasping the full meaning of Richie's words. He had appeased the boy for the time being, but not for long. Richie had clearly conveyed his wait-and-see attitude. The feeling matched that of his own impatience in waiting for the answer from George Weston.

Richie stood up, threw his empty soft-drink can in the trash, and headed for the door. ''I need to get going.''

''Hold on a minute. I'll have Fred drive you home.''

Wyatt watched from the foyer window a short while later as the car disappeared down the long drive. As soon as Fred and Richie were out of sight, he rushed upstairs to check the fax machine. He should have driven Richie home himself, but he did not want to risk running into Vicki until he had the appropriate documents in hand to settle his suspicions one way or the other.

He stared at the fax machine. The catch-tray was empty.

Then, a moment later the machine came to life. He watched as the three sheets of paper settled in the tray. The anxiety churned in the pit of his stomach as he picked up the cover sheet from George Weston. It was short and to the point, stating the two documents requested were attached and if he needed anything else to call.

Wyatt took a calming breath, closed his eyes for a moment, then picked up the two remaining sheets of paper. The first one was the wedding certificate that simply confirmed the date in the newspaper article. Then he looked at the second certificate. It bore the name Richard Dalton Bingham. His hand trembled and a lump came to his throat as he stared at the date.

He plopped back into the chair in stunned silence. He felt as if all the energy had been drained from his body. Even though he had mentally prepared himself for the possibility, he had not been prepared for the reality. The date on the birth certificate clearly confirmed it. Backtracking that date by nine months put conception at three weeks before his father sent him to South America—the precise time of the beach party when they had ended up making love.

Richie had to be his son.

He forced himself out of the chair. He had the proof he wanted right in his hand. The anger churning inside him combined with an incredible sense of loss. There was nothing left to do except confront Vicki and demand an explanation. Not that it would matter. There was nothing she could say that would justify her keeping his son from him, especially in light of everything that had happened Saturday night. He had thought fifteen years of turmoil had been laid to rest. Instead he found that the woman he loved had dealt him the ultimate betrayal. And it was tearing him apart.

He clenched his jaw. They would have this out right now. He glanced at his watch. It was almost time for the market to close. If he hurried, he could catch her before she went home. This was something that needed to be handled away from her house…and away from Richie. He grabbed his keys and headed toward his car, each step hitting the ground with a purposeful thud.

A few minutes later he pulled up next to the post-office entrance. He waited until he saw her lock the front door of the market and put out the Closed sign. As soon as she went to the back office, he entered through the post-office door.

Vicki had only a few items to take care of in the office, then she would be through for the day. A dull ache had lodged behind her eyes and at her temples and had stayed there the entire day. Then she heard it, heard the footsteps draw closer. She knew it was Wyatt. She had seen Richie in the car with Fred Olson when Fred dropped him off at home. Richie had not checked in with her when he had gotten home from school. There could be no other explanation for it…other than that her son had been with Wyatt. And now Wyatt had come to see her in her office rather than at home and he had waited until the market was closed for the day.

She looked up and saw him standing at the door. The hard expression on his face and the icy glint in his blue eyes sent a shiver up her spine. She knew, as surely as the sun rose in the east and set in the west, that her entire world teetered on the brink of destruction. Somehow, he must have found out about Richie. The only remaining unanswered question was whether or not he had told her son—*their* son—the truth.

Wyatt's voice was under control, but he was not able to keep out the slight edge that revealed his emotional stress. "We have something that must be settled here and now."

She tried to maintain the facade she had constructed, even though deep down inside she knew it was a useless attempt. "I...I thought we settled everything a couple of days ago—your father, my father, what happened..." Her voice trailed off as she simply ran out of words.

He entered the office and crossed to her desk. He held out the faxed copy of the newspaper announcement about her marriage. "I found this very interesting, especially the date."

Her hand trembled as she took the piece of paper from him. She started to look at it, but was momentarily distracted by a noise. She glanced past Wyatt toward the door. It would be just like Alice Thackery to pick this time to check on her mail. She did not see anyone or hear anything else. She looked back at the sheet of paper she held. A sick churning started in the pit of her stomach as she glanced at the item.

Wyatt continued without giving her an opportunity to say anything. "It appears that you had been married only a few months when Richie was born." He stared at her, as if waiting for her to make the next move.

Vicki shifted uncomfortably in her chair as she tried to collect her thoughts. Her need to protect her son brought out her defensiveness. "All right! So I was pregnant when Robert and I got married. That's hardly a crime. Besides, it's no one's business except Robert's and mine."

"Oh?" It was only one word, but it dripped with sarcasm. He shoved the faxed copy of Richie's birth certificate at her. He had circled the date of birth in red and next to it he had backtracked nine months and written in the probable date of conception. "And what about the baby's father, Vicki? Shouldn't it be his business, too?" He fixed her with a penetrating, soul-searching stare. He was not able to keep the anger out of his voice, no matter how much he tried. "I want an answer to my question, Vicki. I want an answer right now! What about my right to know that I have a son?"

She recoiled against the sharp banging sound as he pounded his fist against her desk. She had never seen him so angry, except when he had hurled his father's portrait against the wall. She stared at the birth certificate. There was nothing she could say to defuse the situation, no way she could sidestep the issue or the impending confrontation. She looked up at Wyatt. Her greatest fear had come to fruition. The most closely guarded secret of her life was no longer a secret. She fought to keep the tears out of her eyes.

Her voice quavered at first, then grew strong with her anger. "And how do you suggest I should have conveyed the information to you that I was pregnant? Should I have mentioned it to your father? The very same man who sent you to South America and then informed me you had to get away because I was smothering you? Up until two days ago I thought you had walked out on me. I had no idea where you had gone or how to get in touch with you. This is a very small town. There was no way I could stay here and have my baby. No way I could raise my son here without him being the target of malicious ridicule by people like Alice Thackery. No way could I allow that to happen.''

"All right!" He angrily raked his fingers through his hair, then took a deep breath in an effort to calm down. "All right. So you couldn't tell me at the time. But what about two days ago? Saturday night, Vicki..." He placed his hands on her desk, palms down, and leaned forward until their faces were almost touching. "Why didn't you tell me Saturday night?"

A long moment of silence filled the air, followed by an angry outburst from the hallway.

"What are the two of you talking about?" Richie shoved his way into the office, his face covered with a combination of hostility and hurt. "Robert Bingham is my father!" He glared defiantly at Wyatt, then at his mother.

Vicki's hand flew to her mouth and her eyes widened in shock. "Richie..." Her son had caused the noise she heard earlier, then dismissed. Richie had been in the other room. She blinked her eyes several times as they filled with tears. It felt as if her insides were being ripped apart. "Oh, dear God...no...it can't happen like this." The two people she cared most about in the whole world were both glaring at her with resentment in their eyes.

Richie fixed his mother with a hard stare, but his voice cracked as he spoke. "Why are you doing this?" He glanced at Wyatt, then back at Vicki. The mature young man had disappeared and an angry and hurt boy stood in his place—a boy who was fighting back his own tears. "How come you're saying Wyatt's my father?"

Vicki took a deep breath, then forced out the most difficult words of her life. "Because it's true, Richie. Wyatt Edwards is your biological father."

Ten

Richie's reaction was immediate. "No! You're lying!"

Vicki rose from her chair and reached for her son, but he angrily brushed her hand away, and backed out of her reach.

Wyatt stepped in between them, turning his attention to Richie. "You called me because you wanted to address the situation like an adult. You asked me what my intentions were toward your mother. Well, if you want to be treated like an adult, then you'll have to behave like one. Now, let's discuss this calmly and rationally without all the excess emotional baggage clouding the issue."

Richie's defiance extended to Wyatt. "That's easy for you to say. You knew all about this."

Wyatt grabbed the copy of Richie's birth certificate from the desk and held it up for him to see. He forced a calm to his voice. Directing anger toward Richie would serve no purpose, but in fact would be counterproductive. "All of this is new to me, too. I first suspected yesterday morning. I received this fax after you left my house this afternoon. I've only known for half an hour."

Richie glared at Vicki. He tried to speak, then just gave up and stormed out of the office.

"I've got to stop him, Wyatt!" Panic grabbed Vicki as she started toward the door. "I've got to make him understand—"

Wyatt caught her by the arm and stopped her. "Let him go, Vicki," he said softly. "He's hurt, angry and confused. He needs time to think, to let everything sink in. He has to calm down before you can talk to him. He has to try to work this out for himself." He shook his head in exasperation. "*I'm* having difficulty handling this rationally and I'm thirty-seven years old. I can imagine how hard it must be for Richie."

Letting out a sigh of resignation, Wyatt plopped onto the couch. He might have calmed down a bit on the outside, but inside he still seethed with uncertainty.

After a moment, he spoke. "I don't understand, Vicki. How could you do this to me? I've missed so many years of my son's life. His first step, his first word, his first report card from school, taking him to ball games, going on camping trips. All the things my own father never did with me. All the things I had hoped one day to share with my son. You took all of it away from me." He looked at her, studied the anguish blanketing her features. "Why, Vicki? Why?"

"Why? How could I possibly tell you without telling Richie? Doesn't he have the same rights that you do?"

"All right, then why didn't you tell both of us?"

Vicki's anger mounted. "Until you walked back into my life a couple of weeks ago, there was no reason to consider it. And even then, as far as I was concerned, the fact that you had walked out on me meant you had forfeited all your rights in the matter."

His muscles tensed again. He sat up straight, making a valiant effort to keep his voice calm. "I'm willing to accept all of that, but I'm not willing to accept the fact that you did not tell me Saturday night. We made love, we finally shared our feelings, and all the while you kept something this important hidden from me."

Tears streamed down her cheeks as she tried to defend herself. "Don't you think it ripped my insides apart? Do I tell you first and take a chance on you rejecting me and my son? And what if you had rejected us? What then? There was no way Richie and I could have continued to live here. Or do I tell Richie first and take a chance on him hating me? And for that matter—" her anger increased as did her volume level "—just exactly what was I supposed to say to him? What, Wyatt?"

Her words took on a sarcastic edge. "You seem to have all the answers. Exactly how should I have gone about telling my son?" Her voice trailed off as sorrow overwhelmed her. A sob caught in her throat. "Not that it really matters anymore."

Wyatt was momentarily lost for words. He did not immediately know how to respond to her challenge...or her moment of sorrow.

Vicki did not wait for him to answer. "I suppose I could have had him sit down and just been very forthright about everything. Maybe something along the lines of, 'Richie, you know that nice man who you thought was your father? Well, he wasn't. The kind and loving man who raised you, cared for you and who could not have loved you more if you had been his own flesh and blood—well, forget about him because it was all a lie.' "

She turned until she fully faced him, and glared through angry tears. "Tell me, Wyatt—is that what I was supposed to say to my son? That the man who provided us a warm and secure home just doesn't matter anymore? The man who never once in any way made me feel guilty or uncomfortable—"

She broke down in tears, but managed a few more words between sobs.

"And now I've made a mess of everything. My son hates me…you hate me…" She could not continue. Everything she had feared had now come to pass. She curled up in the corner of the couch, buried her face in her hands and sobbed uncontrollably. She had never felt so horrible in her entire life…or so alone.

Wyatt did not know what to say or how to respond. He stared at her—at the way she had pulled her knees up against her body, how she had wrapped her arms around her knees, the tears streaming down her cheeks, the sobs that wracked her body and filled the air. She seemed so vulnerable. As much as he wanted to be furious with her, he could not stop his heart from going out to this woman who was so in need of comfort—the woman he had never stopped loving.

It was an incredibly awkward moment of indecision, then his deepest, truest feelings overcame his superficial emotions. He sank onto the couch and enfolded her in his embrace. He ran his fingers through her hair and held her head against his shoulder. A sigh of resignation escaped his lips. "Oh, Vicki..." He placed a tender kiss on her forehead. "I could never hate you. You should know that."

She lifted her head and looked up at him through tear-filled eyes. Her voice was half fearful and half despondent. "Why should I believe that? How could I know—"

"Vicki..." He shifted his weight as he tried to find a more comfortable position. His words were tentative, almost as if he had to force himself to utter them. "Do you love me?" He held his breath as he waited for her answer.

"What difference could that possibly make now? I've destroyed everything. Everyone who matters to me is—"

"Because I love you, Vicki." He said it as a simple statement of fact. "I loved you back then and I never stopped loving you. I've always loved you."

"This is the first time you've ever told me that." Her voice was so quiet that her words were almost inaudible.

"Then I'm truly at fault," he said softly. "Maybe if I had told you when I first wanted to, that night when we first made love on the beach, none of this would have happened. We could have been a family from the very beginning...you, me and Richie."

She shook her head as she tried to wiggle out of his arms. "So much has happened—"

He held her tightly so that she could not escape. "You never answered my question." He placed his fingertips under her chin and lifted her face until he could look into her eyes. "Do you love me?"

Her voice quavered as she spoke. "I've always loved you."

"Then somehow we'll make everything work out."

Richie burst into the office from the hallway where he had been listening to everything. "What about *my* father?" He glared at Wyatt, then at his mother. "Did you ever love *him?*"

"Richie—" The shock sounded in Vicki's voice. "I thought you left. Did you…uh…just come back?"

"I never left. What about my father?" he angrily repeated.

Wyatt stepped into the exchange between Richie and Vicki. "I think I need to let the two of you talk. Unless you want me to stay," he said, turning to Vicki.

"No, it won't be necessary."

"I'll call you later." With a confident smile, he gave her hand a squeeze that said everything would be okay.

Wyatt left through the post-office door, got in his car and drove home. His thoughts were totally absorbed in what had happened and what it meant. He had a son, but would he ever be allowed to be a father? He knew Richie was hurt, angry and confused. It was obvious that the boy loved the man who had raised him as his own son. He knew that would not change, and he did not want to take that away from Richie.

A soft warmth settled over Wyatt. No matter how angry, hurt and resentful he felt about Vicki deceiving him, it was all overshadowed by the fact that she had said she loved him. Everything else could be resolved with time, caring and love. But there still remained the matter of Richie. Was he mature enough to understand, accept and forgive?

As soon as Wyatt was gone, Vicki turned to her son. Her voice pleaded as much as her words questioned. "We need to talk, Richie. We need to talk as adults. Can you do that? Are you able to set your emotions aside and listen with an open mind?"

"You sound just like *him*." It was obvious Richie was trying his best to maintain his defiant attitude even though she could see that it was a great deal of show and much less substance.

She expelled a heavy sigh. "Let's go home. We have a lot we need to talk about."

They walked the short block to their house, and Vicki escorted her son into the living room.

"You asked me a question a while ago. You asked me if I loved Robert. Let's talk about that."

They sat on the couch, Richie half sulking and half attentive. She knew her son well enough to know that the sulking was only an outward display of teenage defiance, an attempt to assert his independence. "Robert was one of the kindest and gentlest men I have ever known. We found each other at a time when I really needed someone. He loved me unconditionally. That's a very rare thing."

Vicki grew uncomfortable with the next part of the story, but she knew it needed to be brought out in the open. It was too late to skip over anything. "I did not love Robert at the time of our wedding. I had a great deal of respect for him and cared for him deeply, but it was not love. I did grow to love him, though. And when he died—" a sob caught in her throat "—it left a terrible vacancy in my life. I missed him very much."

"But how could you say you *always* loved Wyatt if you also loved my fa—" Richie stopped in midsentence, a slight scowl on his face. "I mean, if you also loved your husband."

"There are many different types of love. There is the love you have for your friends, for your parents and for your children. And then there is that unique love you have for that one special person in your life. I was fortunate in that there were two very special men in my life. First there was Wyatt. Then there was Robert. And now things have come full circle to Wyatt again."

"How could you love Wyatt and...uh...Robert at the same time? And does that mean that you don't love Robert anymore?"

Vicki reached out and brushed Richie's hair away from his forehead. She allowed her hand to linger against his face. "No, it does not mean that. Robert will always have a very special place in my heart and in my memory...and in yours, too."

Richie did not say anything, but he was obviously deep in thought, trying so hard to sort out everything in a mature manner. He was still scowling as he stared at Vicki. "So what about you and Wyatt? Are you getting married? What about me? Am I supposed to start calling him *Daddy?*" The last question was asked with a decidedly sarcastic tone.

"I can't answer your question, Richie. I don't think there is an answer...yet. Wyatt and I still have things to work out. You and Wyatt need to talk. I don't know what's going to happen. But I do know that everything is out in the open now. There are no more secrets. There are no more fears about those secrets being exposed. We can all try to sort out our feelings, deal with things in a mature manner, and try to go from there."

She brushed back his hair. "I love you, Richie. Your happiness and well-being are more important to me than anything in the world." She stared at her son for a moment. "Do you have any questions that I haven't answered?"

"I guess not."

"Is there anything that you want to talk about some more?"

"No, I guess not." Richie sat in silence for a moment, with a pensive expression. "Not right now."

She studied him for a moment. "You're almost fifteen years old. As you yourself pointed out a few days ago, you'll soon be going away to college. You're too old for me to be making your decisions for you. This is something you'll have to work out for yourself. Richie, I want very much for the three of us to be close...to be a family. But it can't happen if you won't accept Wyatt as part of our family."

"Do you really love him?"

"Yes, I do. I love Wyatt very much." Vicki brushed his hair away from his forehead again and studied his face. "Are you okay?"

"Yeah, I guess so. I just need to think about this for a while." He rose from the couch and walked down the hallway, a thoughtful expression on his face. Vicki watched until he had closed the bedroom door behind him. She had said everything she knew to say. The rest was up to Richie.

Wyatt had told her everything would work out. He had to be right, he just had to be. But without Richie's acceptance she did not see how it could be. Her temples throbbed and she felt a sharp pain behind her eyes from the stress and tension. She took a couple of aspirins, as a million concerns filled her thoughts.

* * *

Richie slipped out of the house just before dawn and rode his bike up the hill to Wyatt's house. He saw the light on in the stables and went there instead of ringing the doorbell at the main house. Fred Olson was grooming one of the horses.

"Do you do this first thing every morning?"

"Sure do, Richie. Don't matter whether the horses have been ridden or not, they still need to be groomed. Kind of like us. Even if we're just hanging around the house all day, we still take a shower."

Richie picked up a curry comb and offered his help. He worked in silence for a couple of minutes, then tentatively ventured a question. "Is Wyatt awake? I kind of wanted to talk to him."

"I'm sure he's up. He always gets up early so he can talk to the East Coast office first thing in the mornin' before the San Francisco offices open."

"I..." Richie glanced toward the stable door, then back at Fred. "I think I'll go see him. Talk to ya later, Fred."

"Sure thing, Richie." Fred watched as Richie left the stables.

Richie hesitated for a moment, his finger poised at the doorbell. He did not have a clear idea of what he was going to say, but he knew he had to do something. He also knew that Wyatt would not be coming to him to talk, at least not for a while. He had heard Wyatt tell his mother to let him go, that he needed time to work it out for himself. He screwed up his courage and pressed the doorbell.

Wyatt opened the door. "Richie!" He anxiously glanced out to the driveway, but did not see a car. "Is Vicki with you?"

"No, she was still sleeping when I left. I rode my bike."

"Well, this is a surprise." He stepped aside, his mind trying to determine exactly what had prompted Richie's visit. "Come in." He led the way to the kitchen with Richie following. He poured himself a cup of coffee. "Do you want some juice or a glass of milk? I imagine a bike ride up this hill would whet the appetite. How about some breakfast?" He noted the expression on Richie's face at the mention of food. He opened the refrigerator door and stared at the contents. "What looks good to you?"

"Well...I am kind of hungry."

"Why don't you tell me what's on your mind while I fix us some bacon and eggs?" Wyatt took the ingredients from the refrigerator while Richie settled himself on the stool at the breakfast bar.

"Well..." Richie's body language told how nervous and ill at ease he was, how much effort he was putting forth to be very adult about what was happening. "I've been doing a lot of thinking about what you said, about what Mom said...but mostly about what I heard you saying to each other when you didn't know I was listening."

"And?"

"And...and I heard Mom crying most of the night." The anguish showed in Richie's face, telling Wyatt just how much it had upset him.

A jab of guilt shot through Wyatt as he shook his head in regret. "I shouldn't have left her alone last night."

"She wasn't alone." Richie's defiance shot to the surface again. "I was there."

"I know. I thought it would be a good idea for the

two of you to talk without me being there. I didn't know what else to do." He studied the expression on Richie's face for a moment, a look that spoke of uncertainty and confusion. "This has not been an easy situation for any of us, Richie."

"Well...what happens now?" An edge of hostility crept into Richie's voice. "Am I supposed to start calling you *Dad?*"

"Not if it makes you uncomfortable." He sat down on the stool next to Richie. "I would be very proud if you wanted to call me Dad, but I don't want you to think I'm trying to usurp that place inside you where you hold your memories of Robert Bingham. He gave you a home, security and love. I would never try to take that away from you, nor would I want to. We're going to have to find our way through this together. I'm very proud of you for coming here on your own. That shows a lot of maturity and courage."

"I guess that brings us back to my question of a couple of days ago. What are your intentions toward my mother?"

"My intentions are to marry her." A little of his confidence began to fade. "But I'm not sure what her intentions are." He took a swallow from his coffee cup. "What do you think? Does that meet with your approval? Are you willing to give me a chance?" Once again Wyatt found himself holding his breath as he waited for an answer. It seemed like forever before Richie replied.

"Well..." he began tentatively, "I guess that's okay with me."

Wyatt breathed a sigh of relief. He could not stop the big smile that spread across his face.

* * *

After setting Richie's breakfast on the kitchen table, Vicki glanced toward his bedroom. The door was still closed. He would miss the school bus if he did not hurry. She knocked on his door. "Richie? Breakfast is ready." There was no response. She knocked again. "Richie ..you're going to miss the bus. Hurry up." Again there was no response from behind the closed door.

She opened the door. Richie's bedroom was empty. So was his bathroom. She looked everywhere, calling his name as she went. He was not in the house. She went out to the garage. His dirt bike was also missing. Her discomfort turned into full-fledged anxiety. Where had he gone?

She raced toward the phone and immediately dialed Wyatt's number. As soon as he answered the phone, she spewed out all of her fears. "Richie's missing. I called him for breakfast and he wasn't here. I don't know where he is. His bike is gone. Oh, Wyatt...I'm so scared. What if he's run away? What if I've driven him away? I'll never forgive myself if something's happened to him. It's all my fault."

"Calm down, Vicki. Richie's fine. He's here with me."

"You mean that you came to my house and got my son without telling me?"

"No. Richie came here. He showed up at my door this morning. We've been talking."

Vicki felt the anxiety drain from her body. "Is everything okay?"

"Yes..." He glanced at Richie who had been following Wyatt's side of the conversation very closely. He saw the acceptance in the boy's face. A feeling of relief settled inside him. At that moment he knew they would be a family. "Everything is just fine."

Epilogue

The autumn sun shone brightly on a beautiful Saturday morning. Wyatt, Vicki and Richie guided their horses along the trail that led down to the beach. They had spent as much time together over the last few days as possible. Wyatt drove Richie to school and picked him up each day. Vicki took as much time away from the store as she could. The three of them had formed a cohesive relationship, one that quickly settled into a comfortable feeling of togetherness.

Richie rode ahead of them, his riding skills greatly improved from the first time they had gone horseback riding. Wyatt and Vicki followed behind. About a quarter of a mile down the beach, Richie reined his horse to a halt and waited for them to catch up.

Vicki scanned the beach ahead of them as they approached the place where Richie waited. She noticed that something had been scratched into the wet sand.

As she drew nearer she could tell it was words rather than abstract markings. Then she was finally able to make out what it said.

Tears came to her eyes as her gaze darted from Wyatt to Richie, then back to Wyatt. She stared at the message written in the sand.

It read: *I love you, Vicki. Will you marry me?*

Wyatt sat astride his horse watching as Vicki read the message. As soon as she turned toward him he cocked his head, flashed her a dazzling smile and said, "Well? What do you say?"

"I need to ask the other man in my life before I can give you an answer." She turned toward Richie and arched an eyebrow in a questioning manner.

"It's okay with me, Mom."

Vicki dismounted, picked up a stick from the beach, and wrote her answer in the sand next to Wyatt's proposal. *Yes, of course I'll marry you.*

Wyatt immediately jumped from his horse, grabbed Vicki in his embrace and held her tightly against his body. "I love you, Vicki. It may have taken fifteen years, but now everything is perfect."

"I love you, too. I have always loved you and I always will."

Wyatt motioned Richie to join them. With one arm around the woman he loved and the other around his newfound son, he said, "Everything I've ever wanted is right here. I've never been happier in my entire life than I am right now. We're a family at last."

* * * * *

The World's Most Eligible Bachelors are about to be named! And Silhouette Books brings them to you in an all-new, original series....

World's Most Eligible Bachelors

Twelve of the sexiest, most sought-after men share every intimate detail of their lives in twelve never-before-published novels by the genre's top authors.

Don't miss these unforgettable stories by:

Dixie Browning

MARIE FERRARELLA

Jackie Merritt

Tracy Sinclair

BJ James

RACHEL LEE

Suzanne Carey

Gina Wilkins

VICTORIA PADE

MAGGIE SHAYNE

Anne McAllister

Susan Mallery

Look for one new book each month in the **World's Most Eligible Bachelors** series beginning September 1998 from Silhouette Books.

Silhouette®

Available at your favorite retail outlet:

Take 2 bestselling love stories FREE

Plus get a FREE surprise gift!

Special Limited-Time Offer

Mail to Silhouette Reader Service™

3010 Walden Avenue
P.O. Box 1867
Buffalo, N.Y. 14240-1867

YES! Please send me 2 free Silhouette Desire® novels and my free surprise gift. Then send me 6 brand-new novels every month, which I will receive months before they appear in bookstores. Bill me at the low price of $3.12 each plus 25¢ delivery and applicable sales tax, if any.* That's the complete price, and a saving of over 10% off the cover prices—quite a bargain! I understand that accepting the books and gift places me under no obligation ever to buy any books. I can always return a shipment and cancel at any time. Even if I never buy another book from Silhouette, the 2 free books and the surprise gift are mine to keep forever.

225 SEN CH7U

Name	(PLEASE PRINT)	
Address	Apt. No.	
City	State	Zip

This offer is limited to one order per household and not valid to present Silhouette Desire® subscribers. *Terms and prices are subject to change without notice.
Sales tax applicable in N.Y.

UDES-98

©1990 Harlequin Enterprises Limited

Sizzling, Sexy, Sun-drenched...

SUMMER SENSATIONS

**Three short stories by *New York Times*
bestselling authors will heat up your summer!**

LINDA HOWARD
LINDA LAEL MILLER
HEATHER GRAHAM
POZZESSERE

Experience the passion today!

Available at your favorite retail outlet.

Silhouette®

Look us up on-line at: http://www.romance.net

PSUNSEN

THE TALLCHIEFS

the beloved miniseries by
USA Today bestselling author

Cait London

continues with
RAFE PALLADIN:
MAN OF SECRETS

(SD #1160)
Available August 1998

When takeover tycoon Rafe Palladin set out to *acquire* Demi Tallchief as part of a business deal, Demi had a few conditions of her own. And Rafe had some startling secrets to reveal....

"Cait London is one of the best writers in contemporary romance today."   —*Affaire de Coeur*

And coming from Desire in **December 1998,** look for **The Perfect Fit** in which *Man of the Month* Nick Palladin lures Ivory Tallchief back home to Amen Flats, Wyoming.

Available at your favorite retail outlet.

Silhouette®